FORGOTTEN

Book III in the *Forsaken Series*

by

Vanessa Miller

BFP Publishing

Vanessa Miller

www.vanessamiller.com

Printed in the United States of America

© 2012 by Vanessa Miller

BFP Publishing

PO Box 26478

Dayton, OH 45426

OTHER BOOKS BY VANESSA MILLER

Long Time Coming

A Promise of Forever Love

A Love for Tomorrow

Yesterday's Promise

Forgiven

Forsaken

Through the Storm

Rain Storm

Latter Rain

Abundant Rain

Former Rain

Anthologies (Editor)

Keeping the Faith

Have A Little Faith

This Far by Faith

1653655

EBOOKS

Love Isn't Enough

A Mighty Love

The Blessed One
(Blessed and Highly Favored series – book 1)

The Wild One
(Blessed and Highly Favored Series – book 2)

The Preacher's Choice
(Blessed and Highly Favored Series – book 3)

The Politician's Wife
(Blessed and Highly Favored Series – book 4)

The Playboy's Redemption
(Blessed and Highly Favored Series – book 5)

ONE

Margie Milner sat in stunned silence as Linda Tiller mumbled, "Enough is enough of this craziness." The woman then began spewing obscenities as she raised herself from the bench.

Margie had been sitting next to Linda in the back of the church while the deacons told the congregation how Pastor Randolph Lewis had been stealing money from the church to feed his gambling addiction. Margie noticed that Linda seemed a bit agitated, but she never imagined that she would start cussing like she was sitting in a bar rather than a sanctuary. Margie could understand Linda being upset. She was ticked off herself, but she wasn't going to cuss Pastor Lewis over missing money. She pulled Linda back to her seat and whispered, "Now, you know you shouldn't be talking like that in God's house."

"Girl, where you been? God been done left this house." Linda waved her arm around, indicating the sanctuary they were sitting in. "This ain't nothing but the devil's playpen."

"What's wrong with you?" Margie asked, shocked that her friend would say such things. But even as she asked, Margie saw the hurt in Linda's eyes. She recognized that kind of church pain, for she had once endured such pain herself, after putting her trust in a no-good man. She'd worshiped him as if he had been her God, did everything he'd asked her to do. When it was all said and done, Margie had been left with nothing but her pain. Ever since she had fallen into sin with that no-good married man, Margie had been trying to rebuild her relationship with God. Although she had only been a member of The True Way for six months, she was deeply troubled about these allegations against her pastor. She had vowed to get her life back right with God, butMargie knew that she couldn't do such a thing in a church that was as messy as this one appeared to be.

Linda got up again. "I just can't keep sitting here watching this mess." She headed down the aisle toward the front of the church, and this time Margie just let her go.

Many in the congregation she had previously attended knew that the married preacher she had been having an affair with was no good. But no one had the guts to stand up and say anything about it. So, if Linda wanted to get something off her chest, Margie figured… 'bout time. Maybe when this meeting was over, she'd go over to JT Thomas's church and get a few things off her chest as well.

But then Linda said, "What y'all gon' do about what this no good dog did to my son?"

"Yeah," another woman added as she stood, hands on her hips and neck rolling. "Y'all know what Pastor Lewis did to my son, too, but all we've been talking about tonight is the money he stole. Is money more important than our sons?"

Margie could not believe what she just heard. Another level of anger seemed to rise up in the church after Linda's comment about her son. And then others began speaking out. If what they were saying was true, then Margie agreed with them. Pastor Lewis shouldn't be put out of this church for gambling—he should be put out for destroying the lives of those boys.

A husband and wife seated on the opposite side of the church leaped to their feet. "We came to this meeting tonight because we want answers. We want to know why y'all would hire a pedophile and then turn him loose on our children."

Deacon Frost tried to appease them, "Now, y'all need to sit back down so we can take this vote and finish this meeting." He turned to Linda and said, "Weren't you thrown out of this church already? What are you doing back? You really need to sit down, because none of this concerns you anymore."

Linda reached in her pocket, pulled out a gun and started waving it around. "I'm not sitting down and shutting up this time, Deacon Frost. I suggest you sit down before you get a bullet."

"Oh my God, she's got a gun!" one of the women in the back of the church yelled.

Deacon Frost and a few of the other deacons backed away as Linda advanced on them.

A few people ran out of the back door of the sanctuary, while others stayed in their seats, watching the action as it unfolded.

As Margie watched her friend wave that gun around, she felt responsible for what was taking place. It was out of order for Linda to get out of her seat and disrupt a church proceeding in the first place, but Margie hadn't stopped her because she felt that it was high time that somebody let these leaders know that they couldn't do wrong and get away with it. But now her friend was waving a gun around and she had to stop her from making the biggest mistake of her life.

Margie inched her way down the aisle.

One of the deacons said, "Linda, please put the gun away."

Now, standing by the front pew, Margie held out a hand to her friend as she tried to remain calm. She said, "Put that gun away before someone gets hurt, Linda. Let the authorities handle this."

"You don't know, Margie, you don't know," was all Linda mumbled as tears bubbled in her eyes and she began walking down the aisle. Her head was held high as if she wasn't about to commit a criminal act.

The deacon tried again, speaking slowly this time, "Be reasonable about this. There's no reason for the gun, Sister Linda."

"I'm over being reasonable. I told y'all over and over again that Pastor Lewis molested my son. But all you did was throw me out of the church for complaining about this no-good dog." She was standing in front of Pastor Lewis now, pointing the gun in his face. "He was only thirteen when you started messing with him. Now my son is a seventeen-year-old drug addict, in and out of the mental ward. But you don't care. All you care about is your sick desires. But I'm not going to let you get away with what you did."

"Shoot him!" another woman yelled from the pews.

"Stand up," Linda demanded of Pastor Lewis.

"Don't do this, Linda. One of the members has probably already called the police. They will put you in jail," Margie told her.

"They can call whoever they want; I'm not going to jail, though." She grabbed Lewis by the collar and yelled, "Stand up!"

"Okay, okay." On shaky legs, Lewis did what he was commanded with his hands shoved in the air.

"Now, I want you to tell these people what you did to my son."

Lewis said nothing.

"Tell them!" Linda shoved him.

Lewis turned to Linda and said, "Please stop doing this to yourself, Linda. Your son is mentally unstable. He's on drugs, how is any of that my fault?"

"That's a lie," the woman who had stood up after Linda shouted out. "Whattin' nothing wrong with our sons before you started messing with them."

"Sit down," Linda snapped.

Pastor Lewis seemed to exhale and obeyed.

"Since, the good pastor here can't seem to open his mouth to tell the truth, I'm going to tell you all what he did."

"We already know. We can get rid of him with this vote. Put the gun down and let's get on with this vote," one of the deacons shouted from behind the table where he crouched down with others.

Linda ignored them as she said, "My son, Mike, was a wonderful praise singer. Saints loved it when Mike led praise and worship. Then this dog came along." She sneered in Pastor Lewis' direction. "He started taking my son out of town to conferences he preached at, so Mike could sing. But after the conference he was molesting my son and it drove Mike crazy."

"You need to stop lying, Linda. I didn't do anything to your son."

Margie saw something snap in Linda, but she was paralyzed by all that had transpired and couldn't move to stop what she knew in her heart was about to happen.

Linda turned toward Pastor Lewis and without saying another word she lifted the gun and shot him in the head. People screamed and scattered for safety. Spinning around, Linda eyed the bystanders. "You're all to blame. None of you helped me. You people left me no choice. Thanks for nothing," she said, putting the barrel of the gun to her head.

Brain matter splattered the front pews. However, the people had already vacated the seats after Linda shot Pastor Lewis.

"Call 911!" Deacon Peterson yelled as he checked Pastor Lewis's pulse.

Margie was still too stunned to move. She'd known Linda was angry when she stood up, but she'd never dreamed the woman was this upset. *Should I have yelled out and warned everyone? Oh God, what just happened here? I don't understand this.*

Hundreds of mourners attended Pastor Lewis's funeral, including Margie. Since the vote to fire him had not been cast before his death, the leadership of The True Way thought it best to have his funeral at the church Pastor Lewis had led for almost ten years. He had been laid to rest in the purple and gold preacher's robe he normally wore in the pulpit. Pastors from all over the world spoke at the service. They all proclaimed how great a man Pastor Lewis was and cried over the fact that he had been so violently cut down in his prime.

What about the other victims of this tragedy? Margie wondered if any of these men of the cloth had cried for Linda and her son. Would they come to Linda's funeral and say such glowing words over her body? What Linda had done was wrong. There was no question about that, but what Pastor Lewis had done to Linda's son was wrong, also. Margie could make no sense of the whole matter; could find no justice in any of it.

The next day as she sat in a funeral home with no more than fifty people in attendance, Margie wondered why more of the members of The True Way hadn't shown up for Linda Tiller as they had for Pastor Lewis. There were no glowing testimonials spoken over Linda's body. Each person who stood up, from her daughter, Elaine and her son, Mike, on down to friends of the family, only spoke of the tragedy that became Linda's tortured life.

Half way through the funeral, Margie began to cry uncontrollably. It was a bit embarrassing, because she was crying harder than the family members. But Linda's story had touched her in a way that made her want to take action. But what could she do? Linda was already dead.

Linda's sister, Deneen was the last person to speak. She was one of the deaconesses at The True Way. Deneen wiped the tears from her eyes as she said, "All my sister wanted was for somebody to listen to her. She was so filled with hatred and bitterness over what happened to Mike, but she couldn't find any place to release her anger, because no one would listen."

Deneen got choked up and couldn't finish. Mike hugged his aunt and walked her back to her seat. It was at that moment that Margie realized something. Although it seemed as if the church members had turned their backs on Linda in her time of need, the problem went deeper than that. They hadn't just turned their backs on her, they had forgotten about her and just hoped that she would go away and leave them alone.

As Margie and the rest of the mourners filed out of the funeral home, she determined that she would never forget what happened to Linda and her family in the house of God. She would find a way to help other wounded and broken-hearted souls that the church had mercilessly cast away.

TWO

*W*hat becomes of the broken hearted? Well, I guess my question is a little deeper than that. What happens to people after being wounded in church? Those were the words Margie typed into her, "What's on your mind" box on Facebook. She hit enter, and as her post went out to the two thousand and twenty one friends she had acquired on the social network, she leaned back in her chair and pondered the question. Years ago, her broken heart had caused her to leave Faith Outreach, and move in with a loser guy who couldn't spell the word j-o-b. Marissa had been the only bright spot in her downward descent. Yes, she was an unwed mother, and yes, Tony Sams, Marissa's father was now in jail because he refused to get a job and pay his child support, but she wouldn't trade Marissa for anything.

So maybe God wanted her to help others find the bright spot in their pain, also. Her mother had once told her that people go through things so that they can come out on the other side and help pull the next person through.

A ding sounded on her computer, alerting her to a response to her question. She opened the Facebook user's email and read, "They kill themselves; that's what happened to my daughter. Her husband left her for the church secretary, so she swallowed a bunch of pills and died."

With a heavy heart, Margie sniffed and turned her computer off after reading that comment. She went to her bedroom and knelt down on her knees and prayed for guidance and strength. After watching Linda take her own life, the last thing Margie wanted to read about was another suicide. "Lord, I truly want to help, but what do I know? I'm the same woman who got herself mixed up with a married preacher, remember? And let's not forget that I'm an unwed mother. I haven't made the best choices with my life, so how can I help others to make the right choices?"

"Help my children."

Margie heard those words in her spirit, but was still unsure as to how she could help anyone. "What if I run into more suicidal people, Lord? I just don't know if I can handle it. That whole thing with Linda was too intense."

As Margie told God all the reasons why she wasn't fit to help anyone, He simply repeated, *"Help my children."*

Then God opened her eyes and she began to see that hurting people were just like her. They had gotten themselves entangled in some things that they didn't know how to get out of. And if it hadn't been for Margie's mother, loving her in spite of the things she had done and taking the time to pray for her and help guide her back to the Lord, Margie didn't know where she and Marissa would be right now.

Her life might not be totally together. Due to the current recession, she had just lost another job, and consequently she and Marissa were now living with her mother. But that was okay, because Margie had learned to trust God through these hard times. She got off her knees and went back into the home office as she realized that God wanted her to help others learn to trust Him through their tough situations.

Returning to her computer, she logged back onto Facebook and was surprised to see nearly a hundred responses. Deneen's words ran through her head as she read one heartbreaking story after another: *Linda just wanted someone to listen to her.* Maybe other people would feel better and begin to heal if they knew someone was willing to listen to them.

But Margie didn't know how she would be able to keep up a dialogue with the people she wanted to reach. Posting a comment every now and then on Facebook was okay, but if people weren't interested in what she was asking, they would just stop responding. Margie wanted to find a way to engage the people who really needed someone to listen to them.

"How long are you going to hide out in this room?" Betty, Margie's mother asked as she entered the home office.

"I'm trying to get some work done while Marissa is napping," Margie said. She put her elbows on the table and massaged her temples.

"Still sending out resumes?"

"Not tonight. I've been trying to figure out how I can communicate with people who have been hurt while attending church. But all I've been able to do is send out a question on Facebook."

"Well, maybe that was enough." Betty took a seat next to Margie.

Margie shook her head. "I feel like God wants me to help these people. He just hasn't shown me how I should go about doing it, yet."

"I don't want to sound like a pessimist, but how are you going to help these people when you've made a lot of mistakes yourself?"

That was Betty Milner, always saying exactly what she thought, without recognizing how her words hurt. When she was a child, Margie used to think her mother was too cruel to be a Christian. As she got older she realized she had been wrong in her assumption. Betty was a realist, someone who saw the world and the people in it as they were... no rose-colored glasses needed. Therefore, Margie's response was non-defensive. "I was praying about that. I reminded God how unworthy I am for such a mission. But by the time I finished my prayer, I realized something."

"I'm waiting," Betty eagerly urged her.

"Remember how the Apostle Paul kept asking God to take away a certain thorn in his flesh?"

"Yes, I know that scripture well. I've lived it," Betty said with sorrow etched across her face.

"Well, what if his thorn in the flesh was something that others could point to and ridicule him about? I mean, think about it, Mama. Apostle Paul could have been dealing with something that others could have used to show why he was unfit for the ministry. But God simply told him, 'My grace is sufficient for you.' So maybe God's grace is sufficient for me in this situation, also."

"You better preach, girl," Betty said as she stood up and patted Margie on the back. "Forget about what I said, Margie. You just go on and let God use you."

"I'm trying, Mama, I really am. Through Linda, God showed me that there are people out there with worse pain than I endured, but they have been cast aside and forgotten by the very people who are supposed to go out and get the lost... I just want to help," she sighed, "be a listening ear or something. I'm just praying that God will help me with this."

"If He is calling you to do this, then He will. Plus, I'm here for you." Betty headed for the door.

Before her mother could get out of the room, Margie asked, "But how can I reach people that are hiding because of their pain? It's not like I have a platform or a pulpit."

Betty was reflective for a moment, then she snapped her fingers. "What about starting one of them Yahoo groups, or a fan page on Facebook? The online ministry that I'm a member of has both, and we are able to communicate with each other all the time."

Nodding, Margie considered that a real possibility. "Mother, you are a genius. I hadn't even thought about that. I'll call it the 'When Church Hurts Group.'"

Pastor Lamont Stevens was seated behind his office manager's desk opening the mail and answering the phone. Frustrated, Lamont searched through her computer files. He needed the information on an upcoming funeral and the list of members that he visited in the hospital. If he didn't find those files, Lamont wasn't sure how he would be able to meet his commitments for the rest of the week.

His former office manager, Beverly Johnson wasn't about to help him out. Less than an hour ago, she stepped from behind her desk, grabbed her purse and screamed, "I can't take this anymore."

Lamont had no idea what Beverly was so upset about, but honestly, after witnessing one of his deacons get handcuffed and thrown into the back of a police car on the news last night, and then visiting Darla Williams, one of his most faithful members, at the hospital this morning after she tried to commit suicide, nothing else could shock him.

Lamont had started his church at the encouragement of Pastor JT Thomas, his friend and mentor. JT had convinced Lamont that God was going to use him in a mighty way. However, JT had been talking about sometime in the future, but Lamont had believed that his time was right now. So he'd spent most of the money his dad had given him as kind of a very late child support check and opened Overcomers Outreach Ministries.

The name had a special meaning to him, because he was working to overcome some bad decisions he'd made in his life before JT came and rescued him in Louisiana. But as Lamont sat behind his assistant's desk, he wondered if he should change the name of his church from Overcomers to Quitters and Bank Robbers. Lamont just couldn't figure out how people could so easily give up on God and His great gift of salvation.

"Hey Youngblood, whatcha know good?"

Lamont looked up into the smiling face of the infamous JT Thomas, the man who got him into this present mess. "I don't know too much good today, since I just had another office manager quit on me this morning."

"You're kidding," Cassandra Thomas, JT's beautiful wife said as she walked into the room behind her husband.

"I wish I was, but obviously I need divine intervention on how to pick good employees," Lamont said.

"I hate to agree with you, but this is your third office manager. And the church doors only opened six months ago," JT said.

Lamont lowered his head. "Rub it in, why don't you."

Cassandra walked behind the desk and grabbed hold of Lamont's arm, ushering him out of the chair. "I was going to attend the lunch meeting the two of you have with Pastor Jenson, but why don't you and JT go. I'll see if I can get some of this stuff straightened out for you here."

Jumping out of the chair with a hopeful look on his face, Lamont gave Cassandra a kiss on the cheek. "Thank you so much," he said with a sigh of relief. "I'm blessed to have the two of you in my life."

JT turned to his wife and asked, "Do you think you might be able to help Lamont out a couple days a week... until he can hire someone else?"

"I'll do better than that," Cassandra said. "I plan to help him find his next office manager—someone who will work hard and be dependable."

"I could kiss you again," Lamont said.

JT held a hand up, restraining Lamont. "Hold it now, Youngblood. I can see right now that we need to find you an office manager *and* a woman, with all this kissing you're trying to do."

"Leave Lamont alone, JT. He has been going through it, trying to get his ministry up and running." Cassandra leaned over and pecked Lamont on the cheek. "He deserves a kiss."

"Come on, boy, let me get you out of here before I lose my appetite," JT said in a disgruntled manner.

Lamont and Cassandra both laughed as JT pushed Lamont towards the door. "Bring me a grilled chicken salad back from wherever y'all decide to eat at," Cassandra said.

"You got it, babe." JT grinned like a man who'd just won a million dollars as he and Lamont stepped outside.

"What are you grinning about?" Lamont asked once they were in the car and on their way down the street.

JT gave him a questioning glance, then as he turned back to the road. "What? I didn't realize that I was grinning... guess it's just the joy of the Lord shining through."

"Mmph," Lamont said with a smirk on his face.

"Mmph, what?"

Lamont leaned back in his seat. "I just think it's nice to have a woman that puts a smile on your face like that."

Grinning again, JT said, "Sanni does make me happy. I just wish I hadn't been such a knuckle head for the first few years of our marriage."

"I know what you mean. I'm praying that I'll know a good thing when I see her and won't get caught slipping, like so many of us do," Lamont said.

JT hit the brake hard as they pulled up to a traffic light. He eyed Lamont. "Did I hear you right? Are you actually thinking about finding a wife and settling down?"

"I'm thinking about it." Lamont had wounds that needed to be healed before he could truly consider marriage, but he was working on it.

"What about Sonya? Have you forgiven yourself for that situation yet?"

Lamont glanced out of his window and counted cars as

they drove by. "I've been praying about it. Some days I think I've finally let it go and forgiven myself, but other days I still feel this weight of condemnation."

"You know God isn't condemning you, right?"

"Yeah, JT, I know," Lamont said. But he still hadn't found a way to get himself out of the prison he'd put himself in, so he switched the subject. "And can you please explain to me why in the world you would agree to do a revival with the likes of Walt Jenson?"

"What do you mean?"

"You know exactly what I mean. The man is no good. He preaches on Sunday, but sleeps around on his wife the rest of the week... and I might be giving him too much credit, because he might be cheating on her on Sunday, too."

"Sadly, he probably is," JT agreed.

"Then why do we need to partner with him on this revival?"

JT shook his head. "We don't need Walt... he needs us. And since I used to be just like him, I want to be there when things fall apart for him. This is just my way of paying it forward."

Now Lamont was confused. "What do you mean?"

"When I fell into sin and lost my church, most everyone left me and called me everything but a child of God. But there were two preachers who stuck with me. They mentored me until I was strong enough to once again stand on my own two feet."

"Is that why you're mentoring me even though I decided to open my own church well before you thought I was ready?"

They came to a red light; JT stopped and then turned to Lamont. "I might not agree with your timing, but make no mistake about it, you are a better man than I ever will be. So, I have no worries that you're going to make the same mistakes I made. I am mentoring you because I believe God has a mission for you and I want to be there to help move you in the right direction so you don't miss your moment."

"Wow, thanks for saying that, JT. I had no idea that you believe that strongly in me and what God has for me."

"Just don't let it go to your head," JT said with a chuckle, then took off again when the light changed. "As a matter of fact, I want you to pay close attention to everything said and done by Walt, so that you know exactly what not to do."

THREE

"Mom, come look!" Margie yelled from the small room in her mother's house that she had converted into an office.

Betty ran through the house and stumbled over her feet as she pushed open the door and entered Margie's office. "What's wrong? What happened?"

"Calm down, Mom, don't have a heart attack. I just wanted to show you something." Margie pointed to her computer screen.

Grabbing her chest, Betty took a few deep breaths as she sat down next to Margie. "You mean to tell me that you were screaming through this house like somebody was chasing you so that you could show me something on Facebook?"

Laughing at her scolding, Margie put her hand on her mother's shoulder. "You can stop worrying about me so much. I'm all right." She lifted her hand scout's honor style. "I promise."

"Girl, whatever. I hope you know that a mother's job is never done. I'm going to worry about you until the day they carry me out of here in a pine box."

"Well, I'm just trying to let you know that God has my back." Margie pointed to her computer screen again. "And this is proof."

Betty leaned closer to the screen, squinted as she read the information and then exclaimed, "You've got a job interview!"

"Yes, can you believe it? All these months of searching the Help Wanted ads, and Internet job sites without even getting a call back... then I'm on Facebook and see a post about a pastor looking for an office manager and bam... I emailed them my resume and I've got an interview."

Betty gnawed on her bottom lip. "You'll be working for a preacher?"

"There you go worrying again." Margie playfully nudged her mother as she said, "I'm not the same person who used to work for JT, Mom. I won't make the mistake of falling for another preacher ever again. So trust me when I say that your prayers worked; I now have sense enough to know what's good for me and what's not."

Betty gave her daughter a hug. "You're right, honey. I should stop worrying so much about you. After all, you are a full grown woman with a job interview." With those words, Betty got up and started dancing around the room. "My baby has a job... my baby has a job," she chanted as she danced.

"Hold up, Mama. I don't have the job yet, just an interview."

Betty stopped dancing, turned to Margie and gave her a challenging look. "Didn't you just get finish telling me that God's got this?"

"Yeah."

"Then you've got this job. It's in the bag, girl. So you might as well get up and start shouting with me."

Thinking that her mother had the right attitude, Margie got up and started her own two step. "I got a job... I got a job."

As she drove to Overcomers Outreach Ministry for her interview, Margie tried her best to keep the faith. She had been laid off almost two years ago with only sporadic temp jobs and unemployment checks keeping them afloat. Actually, floating was the wrong word for what they were doing. Since her mother was retired and living on a fixed income, they were slowly sinking into a world of overdue bills and disconnection notices. Margie needed this job like she needed to breathe and eat and keep a roof over her head.

Thanks to Congress, her unemployment was about to run out, so if she couldn't convince Pastor Stevens to hire her today, Margie's only recourse would be to fast, pray and call on the name of Jesus, because that's all she had left. Marissa would be seven years old in two weeks.

Her daughter had innocently asked for a princess birthday party. Since all the money Marissa and her mother managed to put together went toward bills, there was no way that she would be able to pay for it. Margie was so tired of telling her little girl that there was no money for the things she needed or wanted.

As she pulled up in the church parking lot, Margie said a quick prayer and then got out of the car. She smoothed out her black skirt and checked for wrinkles in her all business white, button down shirt. As far as Margie was concerned, she looked professional. She tucked her portfolio, which held her resume, under her arm and stepped inside of the church. The fellowship hall was spacious with a bookstore on one side, and tables and chairs for dining or socializing on the other side. The space felt warm and inviting and Margie felt right at home immediately. She even liked the name of the church. It matched her story, for Margie was nothing if not an overcomer. The church layout was similar to the last church she had worked at, so Margie walked up the hall and turned right in search of the office manager's desk or the pastor's office.

But as she turned the corner, Margie thought her eyes were playing tricks on her, because Cassandra Thomas, JT's wife, was sitting behind the desk grinning at her.

"Hello, Margie, I'm glad you didn't have any trouble finding the church," Cassandra said as she stood to greet her.

Margie's feet were planted as if someone had glued the

soles of her shoes to the floor. She swallowed and stuttered, "What are you doing here?"

"I've been helping Lamont out until he can find someone to replace his last assistant. I sure hope you're the one, because I'm tired of this job already," Cassandra joked, trying to lighten the mood.

Margie crossed her arms around her chest. "What have you told Pastor Stevens about me?"

"I gave him your resume, but he and I haven't had time for a sit down this week. He's been pretty busy."

"Mmph," Margie said, still planted in the same spot.

"I'm serious, Margie. I haven't said anything about you to Lamont."

"You expect me to believe that you saw my name on a resume and you didn't bother to inform Pastor Stevens about the mistake I made with your husband years ago?" Margie harrumphed. "I don't believe it."

"Believe what you want, Margie, just know this... I don't spend my days dreaming up things to do to people who have wronged me in the past. I choose to move forward." Cassandra moved toward Margie as she continued, "Now it is true that I realized who you were when I got your resume. I also saw your Facebook page and can tell that you are trying to help others who have been wounded in the church, just as you had been. I think you are the right person for Lamont."

Still not sure if she should believe a word Cassandra said, Margie asked, "And why is that?"

"If you get the job, you'll figure all of that out in due time." Cassandra began walking out of the small office, then she stopped and turned back to Margie. "Are you coming? I'd like to introduce you to Pastor Stevens so I can get home to my children."

The last time Margie was this close to Cassandra, they were inside of a court room and Margie had just testified against her husband for abusing his power as overseer of a church and manipulating her into having an affair with him. Maybe Cassandra saw this as her opportunity to get back at Margie for the things she said that day. Maybe if she let Cassandra know that none of that was her idea, then Cassandra would leave her alone... maybe the next job interview she goes to, she won't find Cassandra sitting there, smiling and plotting revenge.

"Look Cassandra, I don't want any trouble from you. I haven't seen your husband in years and I really need a job so I can support my child; so if your goal is to get me to suffer for the things I did, then rest assured that I have already suffered enough. I'm just trying to pull my life back together now." Margie hated that her voice sounded so shaky, but she was nervous. This woman had the ability to ruin her name all over town if she chose to do so.

Cassandra stopped walking and turned back to where Margie was standing. She gently put her hand on Margie's shoulder as she said, "I have forgiven you, Margie. I think it's time for you to forgive yourself."

Margie's eyes moistened as she held back tears that so desperately wanted to flow down her face. Cassandra was right. It was time for some self love and forgiveness. She nodded. "Thank you for saying that. I've come a long way, and I know that God has forgiven me, but I think I still struggle with forgiving myself for the things I did."

"Well now I know what to pray about on your behalf." Cassandra stepped back for a moment, then smiled at Margie and said, "Come on, let's get the job interview over with so you can take care of that little girl of yours."

Wiping her eyes, Margie said, "T-thank you. I really appreciate this opportunity."

"No need to thank me." Cassandra pointed toward a closed door as they continued to walk towards it. "You've got to get through this interview in order to get the job."

She nodded and composed herself. "Right, lead the way."

Cassandra knocked on Lamont's door and then opened it after hearing him say, 'Come in'. "Your eleven o'clock interview is here. I gave you her resume yesterday."

Lamont picked up a piece of paper off his desk. "Yes," coming to his feet, he walked around the desk and extended his hand. "Hi Margie, I'm Pastor Lamont Stevens. Thank you for interviewing with me today."

When Margie's eyes fell on the pastor of Overcomers Outreach Ministry, she wanted to turn around and run out of the church door, screaming to the Lord to deliver her from finer than fine preachers. With his light green eyes and caramel complexion, the man standing before her was the most gorgeous man she had ever laid eyes on.

When he put his hand in hers, Margie could swear she felt the earth move. Or maybe it was just the part of earth that she was standing on. *Run. Run now.*

"Would you like to have a seat so we can discuss your resume?" Lamont asked.

Trying to regain her senses, Margie shook herself and then started stuttering. "Y-yes, I-I'd like to have a seat." She sat, hoping that her part of the earth would stop moving as she silently prayed for strength.

"I think I'll be heading out, Lamont. So, if you need anything after your interview, just call my cell phone," Cassandra said as she backed out of the room.

"Thanks for all your help, Cassandra. I know you need to get home to see about the kids, so I'll try not to bug you today," Lamont said with a chuckle and then turned back to Margie. "I guess it's just you and me then, Ms. Milner."

God help me, she prayed as she said, "I'm ready to get started whenever you are."

As Lamont took his seat, he said, "I've read over your resume and I'm convinced that you can handle the office manager job, so I really only have one question for you."

Oh God, here it comes. Margie's greatest fear was about to be realized, she just knew that when Pastor Lamont opened his mouth again, the question he would be asking would have something to do with her inappropriate relationship with JT or her testimony against JT. She felt like getting up and walking out of the office right then and there, but her daughter's precious face flashed before her eyes and glued her to that seat. She would take whatever Pastor Lamont dished out and then she would beg him for the opportunity to prove that she was a changed person.

"Are you ready for my question?" Lamont asked with a big grin on his face.

Not able to speak, she simply nodded.

Lamont asked, "How soon can you start?"

FOUR

"Run that by me again?" JT asked after Lamont told him the name of the woman he had just hired.

Lamont was seated in JT's home office with a puzzled look on his face. He repeated, "I hired someone for the office manager position. What's the problem?"

"The problem is not what you did, but who you hired. Did you tell her that your church is a sister church to mine and that I am mentoring you?"

When Lamont originally broached the subject of starting his own church, JT had been dead set against it. He'd told Lamont that at the age of twenty-six he was much too young to take on the responsibility of pastoring a church. But Lamont knew he'd heard from God on this one and refused to back down. He even reminded JT that he hadn't been much older himself when he became the pastor of Faith Outreach.

JT had then mumbled something about not being ready for the responsibility at that age either, but then he stepped out of Lamont's way and began helping him to fulfill his God ordained destiny. Since Lamont knew that JT was still watching and waiting for his 'I told you so' moment, Lamont didn't want to admit that he spent little to no time at all interviewing Margie Milner. So he said, "She seemed perfectly qualified, I don't see what the problem is."

"Maybe I'm making big deal out of nothing. Maybe this wasn't even the same woman. What did this Margie look like?"

A grin spread across Lamont's face before he could stop it. Margie was one of the chocolate beauties that took your breath away. She had long hair, but it was those high cheekbones and that devastating smile of hers that could rock a man's world.

"If it's the Margie I know, then I can guess why you have that silly grin on your face."

When Lamont didn't respond, JT walked over to him and popped him upside the head. "Boy I told you before, don't let a big butt and a smile get you caught up."

Lamont rubbed the back of his head. "I-I don't know what you're talking about. I hired an office manager and she happens to be pretty big deal."

"I know that you haven't heard this name in almost five years, so I understand why you don't remember, but Margie Milner is the woman I had an affair with while I was the pastor of Faith Outreach Church."

"I thought you had the affair with Diane, Lily's mom," Lamont said.

Nodding, JT confirmed, "I had an affair with both women, and they both were trying to take me to court for using my power as a man of God to manipulate them into a relationship with me."

Lamont thought for a moment and then leaned back in his seat and said, "That's odd."

JT rushed back over to Lamont. "What's wrong? Did something happen between you and Margie during your interview?"

"Calm down, nervous Nelly. Nothing happened between me and Margie. I just thought it was strange that Cassandra never mentioned anything to me about Margie."

With a dumbfounded expression on his face, JT asked, "Cassandra was there... she saw Margie?"

"Yeah... she didn't tell you about it?"

JT sat back down and picked up his cell phone. Even though Cassandra was upstairs, the house they now lived in was way too big to be hollering from one floor to the next, so he called her. When Cassandra picked up, he said, "Hey baby, can you come down to my office."

"I'm trying to put Lily to bed, so it may take a few minutes," she said.

"All right, if you could just pop in as soon as you can," he said and then hit the End button on his cell.

"I wonder why Cassandra hasn't said anything to you about Margie," Lamont mused.

JT didn't respond. He sat in his seat, tapping his fingers on the coffee table that was placed in between his and Lamont's chair.

Cassandra opened the door, peeked her head in. "What's up?"

"Come in, Sanni, I just had a question for you," JT said as his wife joined them in his home office.

"Okay, but make it quick, you know how these kids are when I'm trying to get them into bed."

"Yeah, and I know that they don't mess with you unless they are having a crazy moment," JT said with a laugh as Cassandra walked over to him. Then he said, "Lamont just told me that he hired Margie Milner to be his office manager."

"Yeah, I know," Cassandra said without so much as a second thought.

Trying to be patient, JT asked, "Why didn't you tell me?"

"I didn't know that I was supposed to tell you about Lamont's office manager," she said with a straight face.

"Come on Sanni, don't play dumb. You knew that I would have advised Lamont against hiring Margie."

"I don't know why. She's qualified for the job, so who are we to stand in her way when all she wants is a job so she can support her daughter," Cassandra's hands were on her hips and her neck was rolling.

JT held up a hand, "Look Sanni, I'm not trying to start a fight with you, but I just can't see how you knew Margie was interviewing for that position and didn't say anything to either me or Lamont."

Cassandra turned to Lamont and earnestly said, "I'm sorry if I've caused you any problems with my husband. But, honestly, I looked over Margie's resume myself and she did seem to be a good match for what you need."

"I thought so, too," Lamont said.

JT got to his feet. "I don't have an issue about whether or not Margie can do the job. My problem is what she might do to Lamont. And I don't want him getting off focus." Pacing the floor again, JT mumbled, "Lamont is a young preacher, he's going to have women coming at him from all directions as it is... so he doesn't need that kind of distraction in his business office as well."

Cassandra sat in the seat her husband vacated and studied him for a moment. "Look, JT, I know that you visit Overcomers quite a bit to help Lamont get things up and running, so are you worried about Lamont being distracted or yourself?"

JT turned and faced his wife. "That's a low blow, Sanni."

Lamont held up a hand. "Can we talk about something else? I really didn't mean to get anything started."

"That's okay, Lamont," JT said and then turned back to his wife. "I know I haven't been the best husband I could have been, but I haven't so much as thought about another woman other than you in the last five years. Now if that doesn't convince you that I'm not interested in any kind of *distractions*, then I don't know what to tell you."

Standing up, Cassandra went to her husband. "You're right. That was a low blow. And I don't think that you're looking for distractions. But, JT, you need to understand that Lamont is a grown man and since he is single, if he wants to date any woman, that's his decision."

Lamont jumped up, hands flailing in the air. "Hold up, who said anything about me dating... I'm not looking for a woman. I have too much to do with my ministry."

Margie put a slice of pizza on Marissa's plate as her daughter watched the singing and dancing Chuck E. Cheese characters that were performing on stage. Marissa had a huge smile on her face as if she were really enjoying herself. Margie was glad about that. It might not be the princess birthday party her daughter wanted, but with a new job, Margie felt that it would be okay to splurge on pizza and a little entertainment Chuck E. Cheese style and call it a party.

"This is a bad idea, Margie... just all the way around bad." Betty interrupted her daughter's musing.

She turned back to her mom and said, "I know this isn't the most ideal situation, but what can I do? Bills have to get paid and I need a job to make that happen."

"I know, baby, I know... I hoped and prayed that you would never have to see that miserable excuse for a preacher again in life. And now you're working for one of his friends." Betty shook her head. "No good can come of this."

"I'm not receiving all this negativity today, Mom. I hope, pray and believe that God is going to bless me and that's that."

"I really don't see what the big deal is," Dynasty Wilson, Margie's high school friend said as she put a slice of pizza on her plate.

"You wouldn't," Betty said as she gave Dynasty a disdainful look.

"Mom! That was uncalled for," Margie said as she threw an apologetic look toward her friend. Dynasty had been a stripper for years, but then she gave her life to God and started attending Pastor Walt Jenson's church. As a new babe in Christ she was vulnerable to anyone telling her things that even remotely sounded as if it might be God. And that's how she ended up as Walt Jenson's mistress and the reason that Margie's mother held her in such disdain.

Betty held up her hands. "All I'm saying is that Dynasty is the last person you should be listening to. Mark my words, Margie. Bad company, ruins good intentions."

Before Margie could respond to her mother's accusations against her friend, Marissa yelled, "Mommy, look at Mr. Munch dance," as she pointed toward the stage where Chuck E. Cheese and the rest of his band were performing for the kids.

When Margie glanced at the stage where all of the characters were dancing, she asked, "Which one is Mr. Munch, sweetie?"

"The fat one." Marissa kept pointing.

Margie looked around, hoping no one heard her daughter call Mr. Munch 'the fat one'. She turned back to her daughter and said, "It's not polite to call people fat. Do you mean the purple character?"

Lowering her head in shame, Marissa said, "Sorry Mommy. Mr. Munch is purple, he's not fat."

"Now, we're not going to turn the girl into a liar just so she doesn't hurt anyone's feelings." Betty leaned over to her granddaughter and said, "Mr. Munch needs to stop eating so many of these Chuck E. Cheese pizzas and then nobody will call him fat... right?"

Perking up, Marissa nodded. "Right. Mr. Munch should eat a salad like Mommy." Marissa pointed to the salad that Margie was eating and then turned back to the stage to finish watching the characters perform.

"I don't know what I'm going to do with you," Margie told her mother as she shook her head.

"That's easy, just love me and listen to my advice."

"I listen to your advice."

Betty looked at Dynasty again and said, "Not about everything."

Dynasty stood. "Look, I'm not going to keep sitting here while your mother treats me like I'm nothing." She hugged Margie. "I'll give you a call later."

"Hopefully when you call, you'll be single and free of all things that don't belong to you," Betty said.

In a huff, Dynasty stormed away from the table.

"That was uncalled for, Mother," Margie said as she got up from the table and followed Dynasty out. When she caught up with her friend in the parking lot, Margie apologized. "I'm sorry about that, girl. My mother shouldn't have said those things to you."

Dynasty took her car keys out of her Coach purse and moved a few strands of hair out of her face. "You told your mother about me and Walt, didn't you?"

Margie backed up, held up a hand as she said, "I didn't tell her anything. I think she overheard one of our conversations."

"Whatever." Dynasty rolled her eyes.

"Look, Dynasty, I haven't made my feelings a secret. I think what you're doing is wrong and you are going to come out on the losing end. But my mom shouldn't have come at you like that, and I'm sorry."

"I gotta go. I'm supposed to be meeting up with Walt."

Margie didn't respond, but the look on her face said it all.

"Whatever," Dynasty said again as she got in her car and drove off.

As Margie went back into Chuck E. Cheese's and sat back down with her family, she silently prayed that Dynasty would figure things out before she destroyed herself over a man who would never treat her as anything more than a chick on the side.

Betty wagged a finger in her daughter's face. "You need to stop hanging around that girl and you need to quit this job."

Margie nudged her mother's shoulder. "There you go worrying again. When are you going to believe that I am sold out for Jesus Christ and there is not a man fine enough to cause me to turn my back on the Lord again?"

"Humph." Betty frowned. "He was that fine, huh?"

"What are you talking about, Mama? You already know what JT looks like."

"I'm not talking about JT, I'm talking about this preacher you're going to be working for who happens to be a friend of JT's." Betty tapped her fingers on the table. "You've told me about everything that happened during your interview, but not once have you even described this man. That tells me that you're hiding something."

"What would I have to hide?"

"How about the little twinkle you keep getting in your eyes as you talk about this Pastor Stevens." Betty pointed at her daughter. "You're practically glowing."

Margie averted her eyes. "I am not."

"Face it or don't face it, Margie Ann, but I'm warning you right now... God don't like ugly. So don't you get yourself caught up in no mess with another jack-leg preacher."

If she lived to be a hundred years old, Margie still wouldn't understand how her mother could read her like a book. But Betty Louise Milner was right. She had been drifting into crazy thoughts concerning the gorgeous Pastor Lamont Stevens. But now Margie realized that she needed to float back down to earth and step away from non-productive thoughts. She was taking that job to earn money, and nothing else.

She patted her mother's hands. "He is gorgeous, Mom. But, I'm not going to lose my salvation over Pastor Stevens or anyone else. Just trust me, okay?"

FIVE

Margie's first week at Overcomers Outreach Ministry was more challenging than she thought it would be. She kept her head down and concentrated on doing her work as she tried not to get in Pastor Lamont Steven's way. The man could become a distraction if she let him, but Margie didn't intend to let that happen. Every time she got sidetracked after talking with Pastor Stevens and started dreaming about happily ever afters, Margie simply focused on how horror stricken her mom's face had looked the day she discovered that Margie had been carrying on an affair with the married pastor of the church Betty had been attending for over thirty years.

Margie's mom had been at Faith Outreach when Bishop Turner had presided over it. She'd heard the rumors about him carrying on with some of the women in the church, but had never paid it one bit of attention. But then Margie confessed to her mother that she'd had an affair with JT. After that, the truth had come out about JT and all of his womanizing, and when Diane Benson had taken JT to court, it had also come out that Bishop Turner was Cassandra's father.

By that time, Betty had decided to leave Faith Outreach and had been floundering around looking for a church home ever since. But for one reason or another, she always seemed to find something wrong with each church she attended. Margie felt as if she was to blame for her mother's loss of faith in humanity. And she was striving hard to make sure that she never did anything else that would cause her mother to drift further away from the church. Her plan was going good until Thursday when JT Thomas showed his face at Overcomers. He walked right past her without so much as a, 'How are you doing?'. Margie didn't mind that so much, because she wanted to stay as far away from JT as possible. But then, not five minutes after JT stepped into Pastor Steven's office, Diane Benson, JT's baby mama, came tearing through the place, screaming at the top of her lungs.

"JT, I know you're here. You might as well get on out here and face me."

Margie stood up and rushed over to Lamont's office. She hated the thought of protecting JT from anyone, but she couldn't allow Diane to just barge into Pastor Lamont's office. "Wait Diane, wait," Margie called out as Diane attempted to pass her office, enroute to Pastor Lamont's office.

Diane swung around to face Margie. The look on her face indicated that she was about ready to leave a few pieces of her mind at Margie's doorstep, but as she noticed who was standing in front of her, she stopped, put her hand on her hip and said, "Margie? Girl, what are you doing here?"

"I work here."

Diane laughed. She pointed towards Pastor Lamont's office door. "For JT's little flunky... please tell me you're joking."

"Would you mind stepping into my office for a moment?" Margie asked, in an attempt to get Diane as far away from Pastor Lamont's office as possible.

She followed Margie into her office, snapping her fingers as if she was on to something. "Don't tell me you've got a thing going on with JT again."

Appalled, Margie swung back around. "How could you say

something like that? You know that I don't want anything to do with JT."

Glancing around the room, Diane said, "You've got a funny way of showing it. Because if I didn't want anything to do with him, I sure wouldn't be working for a man he's mentoring... who is more like a son to him than a friend."

"I didn't know that when I answered the employment ad, but I do need a job and I am not about to let JT take one more thing away from me," Margie said with her arms folded across her chest defiantly.

"Well, look at you... I guess you done went and got yourself a backbone, huh?"

Diane was referring to the court case Diane had against JT and the fact that Margie had backed out. Margie knew that Diane thought that she was scared and pathetic for not standing up to JT.

In actuality, Margie hadn't wanted anything to do with the case because she was becoming bitter and angry at a time when she was trying to live, let live and forgive. She wasn't about to rehash all of that at that moment. "Is there something I can help you with, Diane?"

"Yeah, you can tell that no-good, so-called preacher, JT, to get out here and face me like a man," Diane said, raising her voice.

"You just can't come in here and start hollering like this."

"You'd be hollering too, if JT wouldn't let you see your own flesh and blood." She wobbled a bit as she tried to point at Pastor Lamont's door again.

Margie narrowed her eyes and gave Diane a hard stare. "Are you drunk?"

Laughing, Diane balked, "What's it to you?"

"This is a church, Diane. Don't you have any respect for God?"

Diane leaned closer to Margie as she said, "Does he have any respect for me?"

Margie smelled the alcohol on her breath and stepped

back. The door to Pastor Lamont's office opened and both men walked into her office with curious looks on their faces.

"What in the world is going on out here?" Lamont asked.

Diane swerved around, stumbled and then righted herself. "Don't you worry about what I'm doing; I came to see," she jabbed a finger in JT's direction, "this low-down, good for nothing."

"I'm sorry you were disturbed, Pastor Lamont. I'll walk Diane out to her car," Margie said hurriedly. The last thing she needed was to lose her job because she couldn't handle the people who came in off the street.

Margie tried to grab Diane's arm, but Diane pushed her away. "What's wrong with you, Margie?" Diane pointed from JT to Lamont and back again. "They are the enemy. Why are you helping them?"

"This is my job."

"You don't have to explain anything to her. If she had any sense, she wouldn't be coming in here drunk," JT said with a look of utter disgust on his face.

"I know you're not judging me," Diane threw back. "You're the last person that should judge anybody."

"Okay, Diane, you're right. I'm the last person that should judge anybody. Now that you've had your say, can you just please leave Lamont's church and stop embarrassing yourself?" JT still looked as if he'd tasted some sour milk.

"I want to see my daughter," Diane screamed in his face. "You can't keep my little girl from me. I'm her mother, not Cassandra."

"The courts have given you visitation rights, Diane. You're supposed to see Lily the second weekend of every month, but somehow you always have an excuse as to why you can't pick her up when your weekend comes around."

"I want to take her to a party this weekend, but your awful wife told me I can't have her." Diane let out a bitter laugh. "I should have known better than to get involved with you."

"Let me take you to your car," Lamont said as he walked over and gently grabbed Diane's arm and walked her out of the office.

"I don't want to leave. I want JT to admit that he's wrong."

"Okay Diane, I'll talk to him and see if they can work something else out with you on visitation," Lamont said as he continued escorting her to the back door.

In an effort to get as far away from JT as possible, Margie rushed back behind her desk, sat down and began going through the paperwork on her desk as if baby mamas came into the church every day starting trouble with the preachers they used to sleep with.

"I'm sorry you had to witness that," JT said as he stood in front of her desk.

Margie ignored him, just kept working and praying that he would evaporate.

But he didn't evaporate. In fact, after standing there for a moment, he spoke to her again. "I know this is a little awkward for you, but Lamont thinks that you're doing a great job, so I believe that you and I can find a way to get along."

Was this man really standing there lecturing her about getting along, with his raggedy self? She put her paperwork down and glared at him as she said, "Maybe this is awkward for you, Minister JT." She refused to call him pastor after all he did to her and how he left her life in shambles. "After all, here you are a married preacher with ex-lovers coming out the woodwork. That's got to be hard to explain to your congregation."

JT stepped back as if he'd just stuck his hand in a fire and gotten burned. "Sorry for bothering you, it won't happen again."

"Thank you. I'd appreciate it if you'd stay as far away from me as possible," Margie said, with daggers in her eyes. Her venom was even surprising to her, because she had convinced herself that she had worked through all of the anger she'd felt for JT. But having him this close only served to remind her of how foolish she had been once upon a time.

SIX

"Margie, can I speak with you for a moment?" Lamont asked after JT left the building.

"Sure." Grabbing a pad and pen, Margie rushed into Lamont's office. "What can I do for you?"

"Have a seat."

She complied and adjusted her skirt so that no excess skin was showing. "I just finished typing the Sunday program, but I haven't printed it off yet, so if you have any changes, I can make those for you."

"Did you get a chance to put my schedule together for next week?"

"Sure did." Margie flipped a few pages in her notepad. "You have the Joy Given's wedding tomorrow. I'll be here to print the programs for the wedding party and to keep a look out for Diane Benson."

"Why are you looking for Diane?"

"You do know that Joe Benson, the groom, is Diane's ex-husband, don't you?" Margie asked with a glint of devilment in her eye.

"Yes, I know that, but Benson has been through with Diane for years now. I doubt if he would invite her to his wedding."

"Trust me on this, Pastor Lamont, Diane doesn't have to

be invited. The woman just shows up and causes trouble." She turned away from Lamont as she, once again, took note of his golden skin tone and handsome facial features. Looking down at her notes, Margie said, "You also have DeVon Wilson's funeral on Monday, a marriage counseling session on Tuesday and a pre-marital counseling session on Thursday. Other than that, you should have time to work on your messages for next Wednesday and Sunday."

Lamont shook his head. "I hate doing funerals. But so many saints seem to be dying these days that I end up doing two or three a month."

"I know what you mean. The saints keep praying, but the sick keep dying."

"Well, thanks for keeping track of my schedule," Lamont said.

"Not a problem, I'll type it up and add it to your Outlook calendar before I leave work today."

"That's good."

"Anything else?" Margie asked like an eager beaver.

Lamont hesitated for a moment, then said, "There is one more thing that I wanted to speak with you about." Lamont looked at Margie with concern showing on his face.

"Did I do something wrong?" Now she had a look of concern on her face.

He leaned back in his chair, swiveled around and then as he righted the chair, he looked right at her. "I think I should have had this conversation with you the day you started working here, but I didn't want it to come off as if I was trying to get in your business."

Lamont adjusted his seat and looked everywhere but at Margie as if this conversation was painfully uncomfortable for him. "I know that you and JT once had a thing," he began. "I'm not asking for any details or anything, I just need for you to understand that I can't allow your past relationship with JT to affect this ministry."

Margie couldn't explain it, but somehow she knew that Cassandra had kept her word. She hadn't been the one to tell Lamont about what she had done, it had been JT. The knowledge of that set Margie's hair on end more than the fact that she was even having a discussion like this with her employer. "If you think that I have any interest in Minister JT Thomas, I can assure you that you're wrong."

Lamont raised a hand. "No, no, no... that's not what I'm trying to say. I do believe that JT is a changed man, so he's not looking to do anything wrong like that." Margie gave him a look that said, 'But you think I am looking to do wrong?' Lamont caught her look and quickly added, "I don't think that you're interested in JT in that manner any more either. But I do know that you are dealing with a bit of resentment towards him."

"I'm not dealing with anything towards Minister JT."

Lamont looked directly at her as he said, "I think you are still angry with JT—and who could blame you, but I can't have any of the issues you have with him affect the way we conduct business here, because JT and I work very closely together. He has helped me tremendously, and I wouldn't want anyone working here to go out of their way to offend him. Do we understand each other?"

Margie wanted to play dumb and act like she had a hard time with making two and two equal four, but she needed this job. So if he wanted her to treat Mr. JT Thomas with respect, then that is what he would get. "I understand." She stood up. "Did you want anything else?"

He gave her a questioning glance, but then said, "No. That's it. Thanks."

As Margie turned and walked out of Lamont's office, she

kept reminding herself that she really needed a job and that up 'til now, this had been a great place to work.

About the same time, Diane was wishing that she had a great, good or even a bad place to work. No matter what the working conditions, at least she would be getting a paycheck that day. With the child support payments she owed Benson, and with the fact that she was six months behind on her payments and was two seconds from getting a warrant put out for her arrest, Diane needed to change things up.

She had two kids with her ex-husband. Shay and Joe Jr. were both teenagers, so she wouldn't have much longer to pay child support for them. Although the idea that she should have to pay a grown man to keep his own kids galled Diane. But Benson had made sure she would pay, asking that the child support would be auto drafted out of her paycheck.

Once she no longer received a paycheck, the child support enforcement agency was on her back. At least JT hadn't requested child support from her. Although once she demanded visitation rights, the courts had then demanded that she pay child support. At least JT hadn't asked that it be auto drafted, so the courts were only aware that she was behind on her child support for Benson. They had no clue that she had never paid JT a dime in the last five years.

The thought of getting over on JT made her laugh at times. He'd certainly gotten over on her. If it wasn't for JT, Diane would still be married to Benson and she wouldn't be facing the possibility of spending time in jail for non-payment of child support. Diane had recently discovered that child support didn't have to be paid if she lived with the primary care giver. That, coupled with the fact that Benson had moved up to selling Cadillacs and business was booming, made Diane want to go back home like Dorothy in the Wizard of Oz.

She'd been working on getting Benson to forgive her and

allow them to become a family again. Her plan could have worked if it wasn't for the silly woman that he started dating and was now planning to marry tomorrow.

Diane picked up the phone and called her daughter. When Shay picked up the phone, Diane said, "Hey Shay-Shay, whatcha doing?"

"Sitting around here watching Daddy make a fool of himself."

Diane smiled. She knew that the one person she could count on to help her with her plan was her daughter, the original daddy's girl. Shay seemed to hate the idea of someone new in her father's life even more than Diane did. "I know how you feel honey, I can't understand why your father is doing this to all of us."

"Are you upset about this wedding, too, Mama?" Shay asked.

"You know I am. I always thought your father and I would get back together so that we could all be a family again. But then this woman showed up out of nowhere and stole your daddy right from under my nose."

Sniffling, Shay said, "I keep telling Daddy that Joy isn't the woman for him, but he won't listen to me."

With concern in her voice, Diane said, "I hate it when you cry, sweetie. Put your dad on the phone so I can talk to him about this."

"He's not going to come to the phone. He already told me that he didn't want to talk to you until after the wedding." Shay could be heard blowing her nose through the phone line.

"Okay, baby, don't worry about it. Just tell me where your dad is going to be tonight. I'll stop in and talk to him about this situation."

"Dad said that you embarrassed him and Joy the last time he saw you in public. I'm not allowed to give out his information anymore."

This was going to be tougher than Diane had thought. Shay

was going to play this daddy's girl role to the end. She should have called her son. She and Joe Jr. had always had a better relationship. He would do anything for his mother. But Joey had basketball practice tonight, and Diane didn't want to mess with that, because Joey was really good and had the potential to make the NBA... and keep his mama in houses, cars, jewels and purses and anything else she wanted. So, no, messing with Joey's head was not an option. "Look baby-girl, I can tell that you are hurting behind your father's decision to throw his family away for that woman he's only known for a few months. But I can't help you if you won't help me."

Shay cried harder. "I want to tell you, Mama, I really do, but I don't want Dad to be mad at me."

Diane shook her head, she wanted to remind the girl that she was fifteen and really needed to grow up and stop worrying so much about what her daddy thought. Cut the cord already. But if she said that, Shay might also think she needed to cut the cord attached to her Mama, and Diane didn't want that. "Let me help you, Shay. I know that Benson doesn't want to go through with this farce of a marriage. He still loves me and if I could just get him to talk to me, he'd realize that, also."

"I do wish that you and Daddy would get back together," Shay agreed.

"Me too, sweetheart. I just need time to convince Benson of that." She had her now, any moment Shay would be giving up the information she needed.

"Diane?"

That was not her daughter's voice. It was a very angry sounding woman, so, Diane knew that Joy had walked in on her and Shay's conversation. "Give that phone back to my daughter."

"Look Diane, this is Joy and you might as well get used to the idea of talking to me, because I'm going to marry Benson tomorrow."

"Over my dead body you will," Diane retorted.

"I hope it doesn't come to that, but God does work in mysterious ways," Joy said.

"Oh, so you're not just stealing my husband, but now you're wishing for my death also, is that it?"

"No, that's not what I meant." Joy's voice sounded with conviction as she said, "I'm sorry about that remark, it was uncalled for."

Smirking, Diane said, "You so-called Christians are all alike. You pretend to be all concerned about people, while sitting in those pews listening to sermons that God himself isn't even listening to. When you leave church, you wouldn't even give a crust of bread to a man dying of starvation."

"Diane, I don't know what this is all about, but I barely know you, so I haven't done anything to you. And if you are hungry, Benson and I will see that you get something to eat. Do you need us to bring some food over there?" Joy asked meekly.

"No, you idiot, I'm not hungry. I was talking about the fact that Christians don't seem to help nobody but themselves." Diane's neck was rolling as she strutted around her small living room, holding the phone to her ear. "And that includes you also. You knew that Benson had a wife, but you wouldn't leave him alone. Now his kids are being torn apart because of your selfishness."

"Benson was not married when I met him. The two of you had been divorced for four years, and you weren't in his life at all. As far as I knew, you were dating another man as well."

"You mind your own business." Diane snapped and hung up the phone. Diane was fuming with righteous indignation. She swung around looking for something to throw against the wall and that's when she saw Brian leaning against the wall. "Hey baby, I didn't know that you were home. How long have you been here?" She walked over to him and placed a kiss on his lips. Brian Johnson had broken things off with her when he discovered that JT had fathered Lily and not him. But he'd come crawling back last year, and Diane had been thrilled to have him in her life again. But the thrill was wearing off, because Brian couldn't keep a job even if it was glued to him.

"Long enough to know that you're still chasing after Benson," Brian responded.

Diane glanced at the phone that was in her hand; she put it down on the coffee table. "I called my daughter to see how she was doing. Is that such a crime?"

Brian pushed away from the wall. "I told you that I wasn't going to be played for a fool this time, didn't I?"

Standing her ground, Diane protested, "When have I ever played you for a fool? It's more like you're playing me for a fool. You can't even keep a job and I'm behind on my child support because you haven't been able to help me with that in months."

"Oh you've played me for a fool plenty of times, Diane, but I'm sick of it. You can call Benson all night long if you want, because I'm packing my bags and getting out of your life... this time for good."

She laughed at him. "You're not going anywhere. When are you going to realize that you belong with me, Brian? I'm not going anywhere and neither are you."

He turned on her, a vicious scowl on his face. "If we belong together, then why are you still trying to get Benson not to marry that woman? You're trying to go back home to him and leave me out in the cold again."

She was sick of Brian and his inability to understand the way the world works. "Oh why don't you stop whining and face reality."

"And just what is our reality, Diane?"

"You're a boy and I need a man," she said simply, "You're all right to fool around with, but I need someone who can pay some bills around here. So I guess you're right, Brian, you do need to get your stuff and go."

Before Diane could even think about moving out of Brian's reach, he was on her, knocking her down to the ground and pounding her with his fist. "I hate you! I hate you!" he yelled as he kept right on hitting her.

SEVEN

The sky was clear and the sun was beaming down on the church as Margie helped with the final touches of the Given/Benson wedding. Besides the fact that part of Margie's duties included providing services for weddings that were performed at Overcomers, Margie was delighted to help this particular couple because she knew how much Deacon Joe Benson had suffered at the hand of his ex-wife. Margie smiled as she thought about God's quirky sense of humor. Only God could have put a woman with the name Joy Given in the life of Deacon Benson, a man who'd had all the joy stolen from him time and time again by a thankless wife.

"Okay girls, is that everything you need?" Margie asked cheerfully, as she handed the wedding programs to the hostesses.

"That's it. I think we're ready. All we need now is for the bride and groom to say 'I do'," one of the hostess said.

"And since Joy is forty-two and this is her first marriage, I don't think there is anything that could stop her from saying those words today. I'm just so happy for her," the other hostess said, beaming with excitement.

"It just goes to show what can happen if you wait on the Lord," Margie said. "Deacon Benson is a good man, and if anyone deserves him, I would say Joy Given surely does."

With that, the three women walked out of Margie's office. She locked her office door and then headed into the sanctuary to take her seat. In recent years, Margie had begun avoiding weddings. Although they were beautiful, the happy occasion always seemed to remind her of what she didn't have.

She had prayed about her lonely heart; she confessed the truth to God… that she wanted a husband. The rest was up to Him. With that prayer, she had also decided to no longer avoid weddings. Her new job afforded her the opportunity to make good on that decision. So, Margie just wanted to sit back and listen to the music and watch the bridesmaids and the beautiful bride walk down the aisle.

As the music began and the first bridesmaid began walking down the aisle, a woman in shades caught Margie's attention. It was odd to see anyone wearing shades at a wedding because shades tended to dim a bit of the view, and no one wanted their view dim while watching the beauty of two love birds becoming one. The woman turned her head towards the entrance to the sanctuary as the next bridesmaid walked down the aisle, and that's when Margie could see clearly that the woman in the shades was Diane. "What is she trying to pull?" Margie mumbled to herself.

After witnessing her friend bring a gun to church, shoot a prominent pastor to death and then turn the gun on herself, Margie was always leery of people doing strange things inside of the house of God. As the third bridesmaid began her strut down the aisle, Margie eased out of her seat and walked four pews up. As she slid by to sit next to Diane, she said, 'Excuse me' three or four times as she came close to stepping on feet and blocking the view of the bridesmaids.

"What are you doing here?" Margie whispered to Diane when she was finally seated next to her.

Diane slowly faced Margie and then turned back to watch the women walk down the aisle without responding to her.

"This is not a game, please don't do anything crazy," Margie said as she frantically looked around for any sign that Diane was carrying a weapon. Her purse was on the floor, Margie grabbed it.

"Give that back. What are you doing?"

"I'm checking to see if you have any weapons."

"Aw girl, I'm not getting ready to shoot nobody," Diane said as she snatched her purse and opened it wide so that Margie could peak in.

Satisfied, Margie leaned back in her seat. "Then why are you here?"

"That's for me to know, Ms. Margie Milner." Diane snapped her purse closed and put it back under her seat. "Don't think that I have forgotten that you are working for the enemy."

"Diane, please don't cause any trouble. This is Benson's new start. Can't you just let him have it?" Margie asked with a look of compassion in her eyes. She could understand Diane's need to be there. She was losing someone she once loved... the finality of Benson's marriage had to hurt. "Think about your kids."

With venom, Diane whispered, "I *am* thinking about my kids—all of them, and about everybody who took what belonged to me. Somebody has to pay for that, don't you think?"

The 'here comes the bride' music began and Joy appeared at the entrance. Everyone but Diane stood. Joy looked beautiful and at peace as she strolled down the aisle headed toward her knight in shining armor. Margie looked to the front of the church and glimpsed the tears in Benson's eyes as he watched Joy come to him. Margie wondered how Diane could be so bitter about her ex-husband finding someone to bring him such happiness. Couldn't she see the joy etched across the man's face? But then Margie remembered that Diane still hadn't taken her shades off. She probably kept them on so she wouldn't have to acknowledge how happy her ex was. "This is a happy occasion, Diane. Don't do anything crazy."

Diane ignored Margie. She kept looking toward the front of the sanctuary at Benson. Her mouth tightened in anger as Joy and Joe began holding hands. As the music faded, Diane stood and took her glasses off, revealing two black eyes and a bruised cheek. "Stop, stop! I can't let this wedding continue a moment longer." Diane stepped out into the aisle and began walking down the aisle as if she were the bride. "Look what Benson did to my face," she declared before the entire church.

Margie got nervous when she saw Diane headed for Joy and Joe and she flashed back to the day she allowed Linda to walk down to the front of the church and shoot Bishop Lewis in the head. She didn't think Diane had a gun, but something bad was about to happen, a nd Margie wasn't about to let this go down on her watch without a fight. She jumped out of her seat, screaming as if a murder was taking place. Margie dived on top of Diane and kept screaming until someone lifted her off of Diane and took her into the prayer room. By that time, Margie was hyperventilating. The fear of not knowing what Diane would do once she reached the front of the church had chilled Margie to the bone.

"Is she all right? What's wrong with her?"

Margie knew the voice she was hearing was Pastor Lamont. She even knew that at that moment she was wondering why he wasn't still at the front of the church with the bride and groom, but she couldn't find her voice, so she neither answered him nor did she ask her own questions.

"I don't know, pastor. We can't calm her down," one of the hostesses said.

Margie felt as if her heart was about to jump out of her chest. She couldn't stop the heavy breathing and she couldn't respond to the people standing around her.

Lamont dropped down on his knees in front of her. He put her face in his hands and looked deep into her eyes as he gently said, "Margie, listen to me. I need you to slow your breathing down. Just take a slow, deep breath like this." Lamont slowly inhaled and then exhaled so that she could see what he was asking her to do.

Miraculously, Margie was able to inhale and then slowly exhale.

"That's right, now do it again," Lamont said while still holding her face in his hands.

Margie complied and before long she was not only taking slow deep breaths, but she was able to focus on the people in the room and speak again. "I-I'm sorry, I must have spazzed out or something."

"Why'd you jump on Diane and start screaming like that?" one of the women in the room asked.

"I was afraid that she was going to do something to Deacon Benson and Joy," Margie answered truthfully.

"What else could she do?" another hostess asked. "She had already told the entire church that Benson was a woman beater before you leaped on her."

How could Margie explain to everyone her fears, when she had trouble even thinking about the murder/suicide that she'd witnessed in a place that was supposed to bring people comfort and peace... a sanctuary just like the one she had just been in. *Lord help me to get over my fears. I do believe that you are able to protect me and others that enter the house of God*, she silently prayed before addressing the group that stood around her. "It was silly. I should have known that Diane just wanted to cause trouble and not physically harm anyone."

"Well she caused enough of that," Lamont said as he let his hands drop from Margie's face.

Margie instantly felt the absence of his hands and his presence as he stood up and moved away from her. Trying to keep him there with her she asked, "What else did Diane do?"

"She called the police on Benson and tried to get him arrested, but he had proof that he hadn't gone anywhere near

Diane last night. Their daughter also told the police about how Diane was trying to get Benson on the phone last night, but she never even told him that Diane called."

"Did Benson get arrested on his wedding day?" Margie asked incredulously.

"No, they arrested Diane," Beverly, the head hostess said with a giggle. "Apparently, you shouldn't call the police when there are warrants out for your arrest."

"What?" Margie put her hand over her mouth in utter shock. When she recovered, she said, "I missed a lot. I can't believe I lost it like that. Did Benson and Joy get married?"

"Not yet," Lamont said as he headed for the door. "We've already sent all of the guests to the banquet hall for the reception, but Benson and Joy are in my office waiting for me, so we can make everything official. I just needed to check on you first."

"Check on me?" Margie began shooing him away. "After what they had to endure today, don't make them wait another minute."

"You're kind of bossy, aren't you?" Lamont asked as he leaned against the door jam, grinning at her.

"Whatever you say, Pastor Lamont, just go do your job and get those two married."

"All right, all right." As he walked out of the room and headed towards his office, he could be heard laughing.

That night when Margie got home, she turned on her computer and wrote in her blog:

Some days I feel as if I'm standing still and making very little progress. Today I had a panic attack at church, because I feared that someone was about to do harm to another person during a wedding. I overreacted and made myself look like a fool.

Many of you may remember my post concerning the shooting I witnessed at a church I used to attend. Well, it appears that I am still traumatized by that incident and need a bit of prayer

*from my blog partners. So if any of y'all know how to get a prayer
through to heaven, can you please ask the Lord to remove the
entire nightmare that I witnessed out of my mind?*

The next morning, Margie checked her email before getting
ready for church and was stunned to see that she'd received about two dozen email responses to her blog. The first
one she opened smacked her in the face with: I was traumatized at the church I used to attend also. My husband started
spending a lot of time at church working with our choir director on some solos that he felt the Lord had called him to sing.
The next thing I knew, the choir director was pregnant and he
was asking me for a divorce. That's why I don't attend church
anymore... you just can't trust anyone claiming to be a Chris-
tian.No, no, no, Margie wanted to scream. She wanted to tell
this woman that she couldn't judge the entire church by the
actions of one really wrong individual, because many Christians lived right and wouldn't dream of stealing another woman's husband, so she did exactly that, by responding to her
email with the good news that God still lives and He is just
waiting for her to come back to Him.

Margie then opened other emails and discovered that so
many saints had experienced church hurt that traumatized
them. Even if it had been something as small having words with
another saint or having a few dollars stolen out of a purse...
the people had been traumatized by these events because they
never expected to have to deal with such things in the house
of God.

After reading several of these emails, Margie closed her
eyes and prayed, "Lord please help your children move past
the hurt so they can still see Your glory." As she finished praying, Margie found herself giggling at the fact that she had just
asked for prayer for people about some church hurt issues,
and now she was praying for other people with similar issues.

Margie was often in awe of God and His ability to take her out of the messy situations she'd gotten herself into and still find a use for her in the kingdom.

The next email Margie opened brought tears to her eyes. The woman told a story of great heartbreak. The woman had carried on an affair with a married preacher for years. She'd flaunted their affair in front of the man's wife and basically dared her to do anything about it. The preacher's wife committed suicide. The preacher she had been carrying on with for years married someone else after his wife died and the woman who emailed her had since been housebound. Eating her way to five hundred pounds and refusing to come out of the house.

Most people wouldn't have sympathy for this woman. They'd say that she brought all of her misery on herself. But Margie recognized the woman's pain and had compassion for her. She wrote back and said, "Do you know that God still loves you?"

The woman responded with, "I don't feel loved. I feel guilty... like I caused the death of someone who didn't deserve to die. She was a really nice first lady, too. Before I started sleeping with her husband, she used to do all sorts of things for me and my family."

Margie sent another email, simply repeating, "Do you know that God still loves you?"

The woman came back with a question. "Margie, do you really believe that God could love a person like me?"

"He loved King David, didn't He? And David had a man who was loyal to him killed just so he could take the man's wife. So, if God could love him, what makes you any different?"

The woman didn't readily respond. Margie began praying that God would reveal to her His simple truth: That we are saved by grace, not by works. So, even though she committed a grievous sin, she could still be restored back to God. The choice was hers.

A few more minutes of prayer and then Margie received another message from the woman that said, "I guess I'm not much different than King David. Thank you for taking the time to write your blog for us wounded Christians."

Smiling, Magie typed, "You're welcome, but do yourself a favor and go find a church home. The only way out of the trauma is to stand up to it."

"Okay, Margie, I'll do that."

"You won't regret it," Margie said and then signed off.

EIGHT

It was only Tuesday morning, and the week had already turned bad for Lamont. Not only was he still dealing with the fallout from the Given/Benson wedding, but on the same day that he presided over the DeVon Wilson funeral, he'd received word that another saint had been rushed to the hospital complaining of stomach pains. That morning, as he was driving to the hospital to check on Susan Tilman, Margie called his cell to inform him that Susan had passed away.

Lamont didn't understand what was going on. He and every other preacher he knew ministered about the protection of God, and how if the saints pay their tithes, then God would rebuke the devourer from their life... meaning the saints had the ability to live in health and wealth as long as they followed the principles of God. But the saints were dropping like flies on a hot summer day.

After praying with Susan Tilman's family at the hospital, Lamont visited with another family who'd recently lost a loved one. Driving back to the church, he admitted to himself that he was having a hard time keeping up.

But by the time he stepped into the church, Margie informed him that she had already begun working with the Tilman family on the funeral arrangements. She'd also re-arranged his schedule so that he could be available for the grieving family from Monday's funeral and the grieving family from the upcoming funeral on Friday. He had the marriage counseling session that morning, but the rest of his calendar had been moved to next week.

Lamont smiled as he realized just how much he was beginning to depend on Margie. He only prayed that all the craziness around there didn't get to her and cause her to quit like his other office managers. But, really, his other office managers had been nothing like Margie. She seemed to pride herself on doing a good job and anticipating his every need. He wanted to call Cassandra and thank her for helping him find Margie, but he knew that JT and Cassandra were still at odds over her decision not to tell him about Margie; Lamont figured he would keep his joy to himself.

A knock at his door caused him to sit up straight and stop daydreaming about his good fortune. "Come in," Lamont said as he grabbed a notepad and put it in front of him.

Margie walked in with two of his church members following behind. "Are you ready for your ten o'clock appointment with Mr. and Mrs. Cooper?"

"Yes, I am. Thank you, Margie." Lamont waved a hand, pointing towards the couch that sat to the left of his desk.

Stephanie Cooper strutted over to the couch as if she were on a runway, modeling the highest fashions in Italy, while Marcus Cooper stood next to Margie, shaking his head at her. He then nudged her shoulder and said, "Mr. Cooper, huh? What happen to Marcie-Markie the stinking larky?"

Margie giggled. "You did used to stink, with all that gas you kept passing."

"Yeah, but you didn't have to bust me out in front of everybody like that." He turned to his wife and pointed at Margie. "I actually had a crush on this one until she went around telling everyone how stinking I was."

Margie shoved Marcus. "Hey, I was only six years old. What did you expect from me?"

"You called it right, Margie. He's still passing a bunch of gas," Stephanie said with a lot less humor than Margie and Marcus experienced as they walked down Memory Lane.

"Well, I'll leave you two with Pastor Lamont," Margie said and then closed the door behind her.

Lamont sat in his chair for a moment, staring at the closed door. For some reason he had wanted to hear more about this crush Marcus had on Margie back in the day. But the couple hadn't come to him to talk about Margie. "So, Stephanie," Lamont stood and walked around his desk. "When you made the appointment, you mentioned something about problems that you and Marcus were having..."

"That's kind of putting it mildly," Stephanie said as she adjusted herself in her seat. Marcus sat down next to his wife and put his hand on her leg. She pushed it away.

Lamont sat down in the chair in front of the couch. He folded his hands, one on top of the other as he tried to figure this couple out. Lamont saw Marcus and Stephanie Cooper in church together every Sunday. Stephanie also attended Wednesday night Bible study. They seemed happy when Lamont saw them... always walking to the offering basket or to communion holding hands and smiling at each other. "Let's pray before we begin our discussion," Lamont said as he bowed his head. "Lord, we thank You for grace and mercy. I thank You because You know all things and can reveal them to us as needed. My prayer right now, Lord Jesus, is that the Coopers dig deep and begin to reveal the things that are stopping them from becoming all that You designed for them to be to each other... in Jesus' name I pray this prayer and believe that You hear me and are a God that answers prayers. Amen."

When Lamont finished, he looked up and found tears

streaming down Marcus's face. "Is there something you'd like to share, Brother Marcus?"

Marcus held up a hand and shook his head.

"See," Stephanie said frustration filling her voice. "This is the problem. I know that something is wrong, but every time I ask, he just shuts me out."

"I don't mean to shut you out, Stephanie. I just don't want to hurt you."

"Pastor, I just about can't take this anymore. Would you please ask my husband how his telling me what is on his mind would hurt me?"

"She makes a good point, Marcus. A married couple should be able to talk about the things that concern them." Remembering something JT had said about his marriage, Lamont added, "A good friend once told me that trust in a marriage is the glue that binds."

"I do trust Stephanie. I just don't want to hurt her." Marcus wiped the tears from his face.

Stephanie handed him some tissue and he blew his nose. "Why do you think you'll hurt me? I just don't understand when you speak in riddles like this."

Marcus looked at his wife with compassion. He opened his mouth to speak, but then turned away from her. "When you look at me like that, I don't know how to say what I need to say to you."

"When I look at you like what? Like I love you and want to help you get through whatever you're going through?" She grabbed his arm and turned him back to face her. "I look at you like that because I feel that way, Marcus. From the day we got married five years ago, I vowed that I was in this for the good and the bad. But you've got to help me out here. I can't help you get through whatever this is, if you won't talk to me."

Instead of answering, Marcus stood up and walked over to the window. He stood there for the longest time peering out of the window.

"I don't know what to do anymore, Pastor Lamont." Stephanie pointed at Marcus. "He wants me to pretend that everything is just wonderful between us, when he hasn't even touched me in over a year."

Marcus angrily turned away from the window and yelled at his wife, "Shut up, Stephanie!"

"I will not be quiet." Stephanie turned back to Pastor Lamont and continued. "Even before this year long drought, I knew that Marcus wasn't interested in me in that way. Other newlyweds would complain to me about their husband wanting sex a few times a day, while I had to buy all kinds of alluring nightgowns and entice my husband to have sex with me just once a week."

"That's not true," Marcus shouted. "I have a very demanding work schedule and you know it."

Stephanie ignored him and kept speaking to Pastor Lamont. "What I know is that our lovemaking went from once a week to once a month, then once every other month until it just stopped. So, I know he's not attracted to me."

Lamont found that very hard to believe. Stephanie Cooper was beautiful, with a golden personality to match. He'd often thought that Marcus had to be one of the most blessed men on earth to land such a woman with beauty, personality and her own finances at that.

"I'm attracted to you, Stephanie, how can you even say something like that?"

She turned to her husband now, the hurt and pain shining bright in her eyes. "Who is she, Marcus? Why don't you just admit that you've fallen in love with someone else?"

He couldn't make eye contact with her. He turned back to the safety of the window and began looking at the street, watching cars go by. "I don't know what you're talking about."

Stephanie got up and walked over to her husband. She took his face in her hands and she gently asked, "Who is she, Marcus? Tell me the truth."

Tears streamed down Marcus's face as he looked at his wife. His lips trembled as he said, "I don't want to hurt you."

"You already have, so just tell me the truth and be done with it."

He removed her hands from his face and sat back down on the couch with a tortured look on his face. He closed his eyes and then jumped as if a waterboarding had jolted him back into reality. "Everybody wants me to tell the truth and be truthful about who I am. But the truth is not so simple."

Lamont silently prayed that Marcus didn't close down again, before he could release himself from whatever it was that had him bound. "The truth will set you free, Brother Marcus. Don't you want to be free?"

Marcus looked at Lamont, sorrow etched across his face as he said, "I've never been free. I've always had to hide who I really am."

"Who are you, Marcus?" Lamont asked, determined to get to the bottom of this situation.

"I am not the man that Stephanie needs me to be."

Stephanie threw up her hands. "Here we go with these riddles again." She walked over to her husband and sat down next to him. "Will you just spill it already?"

"All right! All right." Marcus's hands went to his head as he shook away the frustration. "You want the truth, here it is. I'm not in love with another woman. I'm in love with my business partner, Cohen."

"Cohen?" Confused, Stephanie said, "But Cohen is a man."

"You wanted the truth. Well I'm giving it to you." Marcus stood up and said, "Cohen and I plan to move our business to Maryland or some other state where we can get married and live as a couple. I've been trying to tell you about my plans for years now, but couldn't muster the courage."

There was a look of relief on Marcus's face as he loudly proclaimed that he wanted to marry another man. But Lamont's and Stephanie's faces had contorted into shock and dismay. Before Lamont could recover from the shock, Stephanie jumped up and started swinging her purse like a wild woman, connecting it to Marcus's head with each swinging blow.

"How dare you stand there and tell me that you'd rather be with a man, than with me," she shouted as she continued flinging her purse and her fist.

As Marcus bobbed and weaved, trying to get away from Stephanie, Lamont stood, trying to break up the fight, but Stephanie was in full swing mode and wasn't about to let her victim go so easily.

The office door swung open and Margie came running. She grabbed Stephanie, pulling her away from Marcus, while Lamont held Marcus back, just in case he was mad enough to fight back by then. Instead, Marcus dropped down to the floor and cried like a baby.

Stephanie was fighting against the hold Margie had on her, and was about to break free, so Lamont grabbed her. "This is not the way to handle this, Stephanie. Now please calm down."

"Calm down? Didn't you hear what he said?" Stephanie pushed and pulled to try to get free. "This man has been putting my life in jeopardy by sleeping with a man while he's married to me."

"Didn't you say that you haven't slept together in over a year?" Lamont reminded her.

"What difference does that make? I could have something that's been sitting dormant for all I know."

Lamont sat Stephanie down on the couch as he reasoned with her. "Make yourself a doctor's appointment so you can get checked out. We will be praying for you and my hope is that all will be well."

"Hmm." Stephanie shook her head. "Don't pray for me. I'm tired of getting prayer at church and having it amount to nothing." She glanced over at Marcus with hatred in her eyes.

"I received prayer before I married him and look how that turned out."

"God has not forgotten you, or your prayers, Stephanie, you've got to believe that."

Stephanie grabbed her purse and stormed out of Lamont's office. "I never want to see Marcus or anyone in this church again," she said and kept walking out the building.

Noticing Marcus on the floor crying, Margie knelt down next to him. "What did you do, Marcus, what did you do?"

Marcus looked up at Margie and simply said, "I told her that you were right. I really do stink."

Lamont silently observed how Margie ministered to her old friend.

As they rocked on the floor together she declared, "God has something better for you, Marcus. You've just got to be strong enough to grab hold of it."

"But I'm not strong, Margie. I never have been... you know that."

Lamont handed tissues to both Marcus and Margie and he waited a while before speaking, feeling in his heart that Marcus needed the comfort that Margie was giving him. When they seemed to be all cried out, Lamont said, "Marcus, can you have a seat, so we can talk before you leave my office."

Marcus looked at Margie and asked, "Will you stay?"

She nodded. "I'm here for you."

They sat on the couch while Lamont continued to look dumbfounded by the situation. Since he was the pastor, however, he felt compelled to say something at this moment. But all he could think to say was, "I guess I just don't understand. You and Stephanie always seemed so happy together. A-And you don't act gay, so I never would have thought that you were struggling with homosexuality."

"All gay men don't run around twisting and acting womanly. I was an athlete all through high school and college, so there was no way I would have gotten away with acting like that."

Lamont rubbed his temples. He didn't know what to say or do. One day he's dealing with bank robbing deacons and quitting office managers, and now he was expected to deal with a gay man who tried to play it straight by marrying a woman. He hated to admit it, but maybe JT had been right when he suggested that he wait a while before becoming the pastor of his own church. "I guess I just don't understand," Lamont repeated.

"Pastor Lamont, there is something that you don't know about Marcus," Margie began. She then turned to Marcus and said, "And if he will permit me, I'd like to shed some light on this situation."

"Would that be all right with you, Marcus?" Lamont asked, praying that he would say yes, so that Lamont could get a better understanding of the present situation. As far as Lamont was concerned, two and two added to four when Marcus, the athlete, married Stephanie, the beautiful model. Now he's talking about he'd rather have a man than the beautiful woman he already had. It just didn't make sense.

Marcus nodded and then Margie turned to Lamont and said, "Let me get you a glass of water, and you get comfortable in your seat, because this is not going to be a pretty story that I have to tell."

NINE

"When Marcus and I were younger we attended the same church. There was a predator at our church and, unfortunately, he was in leadership."

As Margie talked, Marcus seemed to fold within himself. He was there in the office with them, but it seemed as if his eyes had drifted off someplace else.

"This man was thought of as a good guy around the community because he coached little league football and baseball and helped out by buying the uniforms the kids needed and paying for sports camp when a family couldn't afford it. But he wasn't doing all of this out of the kindness of his heart or good Christian charity.

"He raped countless little boys and destroyed their lives. And then one day, I went to that man's church with a friend of mine to give her moral support. I knew that this pastor had molested her son, and that her son was dealing with psychiatric problems because of it, but I had no idea that she brought a gun to church with her that day." Margie paused as she shook her head. "But she had, and I sat in that church and watched as my friend murdered that pastor for what he had done to her son and then she turned the gun on herself."

"I'm glad she shot him," Marcus said with the sound of vengeance in his voice.

Margie turned to him and asked, "Did it take away any of the pain you endured?"

Marcus thought about the question for a moment and then lowered his head and shook it.

"The one thing that I have learned with all that I have been through is that even when the hurt comes from within the church, vengeance still belongs to God. It's His job to repay the evil that we have endured," Margie said like a woman who had learned something while traveling through this life.

"I'm still glad he got it the way he did," Marcus admitted.

Lamont knew the pastor that Margie was talking about. He had met the man a few years back at a revival. He preached the congregation so happy that they eagerly jumped in the offering line for the second time that night. Lamont had not been impressed; he'd known that pastor's motives had not been in line with God, but in lining his own pockets with that second call for an offering. And now he discovered that the man had not only been greedy, but a pedophile as well.

Marcus had Lamont's sympathy for what had been done to him. But Lamont couldn't help but wonder where Marcus's sympathy had been when it came to what he'd done to Stephanie, so he said, "I get that what your pastor did to you was wrong, but don't you think that marrying Stephanie, when you knew that you had feelings for men, was also wrong?"

"I'm not crazy, Pastor Lamont. I knew that I shouldn't have married Stephanie. But she came after me." Marcus shrugged. "I thought I could change and be the man that she needed me to be."

"So what now? Are you just going to give up trying to be the man she wants you to be so you can run off with another man?" Lamont had a hard time getting those words out of his mouth, but he truly believed that God could fix anything. He just didn't know why he had so many quitters in his congregation.

Marcus stood up. His shoulders were slumped as he answered Lamont. "I'm tired of pretending I'm something I'm not." With that, Marcus walked out of the church.

Tired of sitting idly by while the people of God fell by the wayside, Margie made up her mind to do something. She got on her blog and began writing:

> *Church hurt is the worst kind of hurt there is. Because when you think about it, most of the people who come to God have already been hurt in some manner by the world. They come to God looking for a city of refuge. Woe unto the wolf in sheep's clothing who dares to harm a child of God. If that person doesn't repent, it will be worse for him than it was for Sodom and Gomorrah.*

She kept writing as if God was professing through her...

> *The Day of Judgment is not far off. Stop what you're doing... turn from your wicked ways, because it would be better for you to be thrown into a river with a stone around your neck, than to face the judgment of God after having harmed one of his children.*

After writing those words, Margie got up from her desk, grabbed her purse and went to the county jail. She doubted that Diane would want to see her, but even though Diane didn't realize it, she had been harmed by sin in the church and was now acting out because of the guilt she still felt. Margie prayed that one day Diane would repent and accept God's free gift of forgiveness and salvation.

"I can't believe that you took time out of your day to come visit me," Diane said as she sat across from Margie during visitation hours at the Cuyahoga County Jail.

"I just wanted to check on you and to let you know that I've been praying for you."

"Ha! That's rich." Diane laughed in Margie's face.

Continuing on as if Diane hadn't just laughed at her, Margie said, "I feel awful about diving on you at the church last week. All I can tell you is that I had become terrified that you were about to hurt Benson or Joy and I panicked."

"I wasn't going to do anything to Joe. I just wanted to stop him from marrying that woman."

"But you seemed so angry, I just honestly didn't know what you were about to do." Margie doubted that she would ever get over the trauma that she experienced the day she watched Linda gun down Pastor Randolph Lewis. The incident would forever color her reactions. From now on anyone making a sudden move inside of a church function would be suspect in her book. "I just want to apologize to you, because I shouldn't have even thought that you would try to hurt Deacon Benson."

"Great." Diane waved a dismissive hand in the air. "Now that you've cleared your conscience, I guess you'll be leaving now."

"Why do you find it so hard to believe that I actually care about you and want to help you?"

"If you cared so much about me, then why didn't you help me when I needed you the most?" Diane was still angry about Margie bailing on the lawsuit against JT, so she wasn't in a forgive–and–forget kind of mood.

Margie shook her head. "All that happened so long ago, Diane. For the most part, I have moved past all of that. I don't want to live my life being bitter. The way I see it, since God forgave me for all my dirt, then I ought to at least try to forgive people who brought dirt into my life."

Diane rolled her eyes. "That's an awesome speech and I wouldn't expect to hear anything else from a sell-out like you."

Margie had known that Diane would be in a sour mood and

she had decided that she would not let Diane's bitterness stop her from being there for her. "Look Diane, I know that you feel as if I let you down, but I'm here for you now. I really do want to help you. I know from experience the pain you're feeling. But I just don't think you know how to get rid of the pain... that's what I want to help you with."

"Are you sure you won't punk out this time?"

With a look of confusion on her face, Margie asked, "Punk out? What are you talking about?"

Diane pounded on the table and then gave Margie the look of a hardened criminal. All that was missing was the cornrows and she could have been in that Set It Off movie. "I mean that I've got an idea about how I can get rid of some of this pain I'm feeling. All I need you to do is get me JT's schedule so that I'll know where he's going to be at on certain days. You're working on that multi-church revival with his secretary, aren't you?"

"You haven't even been attending church, so how did you know about that?"

"I have my sources, don't you worry about that." Diane leaned in closer, emphasizing her next words. "You just help me get rid of some of this pain I'm feeling."

"How will my spying on JT help you heal from the pain you're feeling?"

"It'll help me to get my daughter back and that will go a long way towards healing all of my wounds. You bet your bottom dollar it will."

Trying to change the subject, Margie said, "I want you to know that I'm praying for you. I've also started an online group for people like you and me... people who have been wounded in the church. When you get out of here, I'd like you to join—"

Diane held up a hand, silencing Margie. "I didn't ask for your prayers and I don't need them. I didn't ask to join your little pathetic group either. All I asked you for was one little favor. So, are you going to get the information that I need or not?"

Diane was looking like she was ready to set it off again, and as a chill ran through Margie's body, she realized that she'd had it all wrong. Diane had not planned to harm Joe Benson. The person Diane wanted to harm was JT Thomas. And although Margie had hoped that JT would one day get what was coming to him, she couldn't be sure that what Diane had planned would be in line with what God had planned for him. So she said, "I can't help with what you have planned."

Diane turned and waved to the guard. "I'm ready to go."

As the guard escorted Diane out of the visitation room, Margie's heart bled for her and for the church of Jesus Christ. How many women like Diane and Margie had walked through the church doors, looking for the love of God, but finding sinful men who aided in turning them into twice the sinful beings they had been before they ever joined a church? How many men were like Marcus... little boys, thinking that the house of God was a safe place to run, play and explore... until they were molested by an adult who professed to love God?

Margie knew that the God she served was not pleased at all with the mockery His son's church had become. She just wasn't sure how many more people had to be victimized before God began getting His house in order. Margie bowed her head and silently prayed, "Oh Lord, please come quickly."

Ten minutes before lights out, Diane was sitting in her cell whispering with her cell mate about the hit man she wanted to hire. "Now you're sure that he has no qualms about killing a preacher?"

"If the money is right, Tony would put a bullet in his own brother's back. The only person he wouldn't hurt is his own mama... yours, he wouldn't have a problem with." Freda said.

"Well, I don't want my mama murdered, just some no-good preacher," Diane said with anticipation in her eyes.

"How much can you pay?"

"All I have is my tax return money that won't be deposited into my account until next week."

"How much is it?"

"Three thousand."

Freda looked worried.

"What's wrong? Diane asked.

"I don't know... To kill a preacher, Tony might want a little more than that."

"Well this one is a jack leg, so I should be able to get a discount, because trust me when I tell you that God won't mind the killing of JT Thomas."

TEN

Lamont was in his car racing to the hospital once again. Margie had called to inform him that Stephanie Cooper had tried to commit suicide and was now having her stomach pumped to try to get as many of the sleeping pills as possible out of her system.

He pulled into a parking spot, jumped out of the car and ran into the hospital, praying with everything in him that he was not about to have to give last rites or pray for the family because Stephanie was already gone. "Please Lord, help your children."

When he reached the emergency room, Lamont spotted Marcus sitting in a corner with tears in his eyes. He walked over to the man and nudged his shoulder. "How is she?" *Please, Lord, please be with us*, Lamont silently prayed.

Marcus's face was the picture of grief as he looked up. "She's holding on. They were able to get enough of the pills out of her system to keep her from drifting away."

"I'm glad to hear it," Lamont said.

But Marcus was not comforted by any of it. His shoulders slumped as a new wave of tears drifted down his face. "It's all my fault."

Lamont sat down next to Marcus and put his hand on the man's shoulder. "You can't think like that, Brother Marcus."

"How can you still call me brother? I am no more your brother than I am the brother of the next man who walks through these hospital doors."

"You're my brother in Christ," Lamont assured him with his hand still on Marcus's shoulder.

Marcus removed Lamont's hand. "Please don't pretend that things aren't different between us now that you know who I truly am."

"Who are you, Marcus? Do you even know for sure who you are meant to be in Christ?"

Marcus exploded. "I'm not meant to be nothing in Christ. Didn't I already explain that to you? I'm a homosexual, that's it and that's all."

Lamont shook his head. "No, that's not it. I believe that we all have choices. You can choose to live for God or you can choose to live for yourself. But make no mistake about it, it's a choice."

Marcus stared at Lamont for a long moment. Finally he opened his mouth, preparing to say something, but that's when a nurse in a lavender smock approached him.

"Excuse me, are you here for Stephanie Cooper?"

Marcus stood up. "Yes, she's my wife."

"Can you come with me?" the nurse asked.

Marcus turned back to Lamont and said, "Despite what you may think of me, I love my wife and would have never wanted this to happen to her."

"I believe that, Marcus." Lamont stood up and asked, "Can I go in there with you? I'd like to pray for Stephanie if she will let me."

Marcus nodded and the three left the waiting room and went to Stephanie's small room. The nurse showed them to the room and then left. Marcus pulled back the curtain and walked in with Lamont right behind him. "Hey baby," he said with a nervous half grin as he beheld his wife lying in a hospital bed.

"Hey yourself," she said weakly.

"How are you doing, Stephanie?" Lamont asked as he stood next to Marcus.

Stephanie looked up at Lamont and started crying. She tried to speak, but tears kept getting in the way.

"I'm so sorry, honey," Marcus said, grabbing his wife's hand.

She pulled her hand away from him and turned her back to Marcus and Lamont.

Lord, help me, I've never had to counsel anyone who tried to commit suicide. Lamont put his hand on the bed rails and asked, "Stephanie, do you mind if I pray for you?"

She waved a hand at him and said, "Not now, pastor... just, not now, okay?" And then she started crying again.

When Lamont arrived at the church, he went straight to his office, sat down behind his desk and laid his head down on it.

Margie had followed him inside his office. She stood at the door watching him, knowing that he was in a battle that she couldn't help him with. Even knowing that, she felt compelled to go to Lamont and put her hand on his shoulder to comfort him. But

since she was not his wife, but simply an employee, she didn't think that action would be appropriate. So, she kept her seat and silently prayed for her pastor/employer. Margie sensed that God was trying to show Pastor Lamont something with all the confusion that had been going on in, not just his church, but in so many other churches across America. She prayed that it would be revealed.

To alert him of her presence, she knocked on the door jam. When he looked up and she saw that his eyes were full of sorrow, she said, "That bad, huh?"

"Worse," he said and then laid his head back on his desk.

"Is there anything I can do?" Margie asked as she stepped into his office.

As Lamont lifted his head again, confusion flashed through his eyes. Then he said, "I'm not trying to get in your business and if you don't want to answer my question, I'll be okay with that."

Margie nodded, wondering what type of question Lamont could have for her that would need to be prefaced like that.

"So many people quit on God so quickly. It seems like they expect life to be perfect for them after coming to Christ, but if they have the least little struggle they give up and turn their back on God.

"But you didn't give up after what happened between you and JT. So, can you tell me what kept you from falling away from God?"

"I wish I could say that I didn't fall away from God while committing those vile acts of sin. But that is not the truth," she admitted. "My affair with JT ended after I called Cassandra and informed her that he was not just cheating on her with me, but with another woman also. I didn't take the break-up well. I didn't just leave JT's church, but I left church and God all together. I then met a man who was just as depraved as I was. I fell head over heels within a month of having sex with him without the benefit of marriage. I got pregnant and then moved in with this man."

Shaking her head at the shame she had brought onto herself and her daughter, Margie continued her story, "My life then became a nightmare as I struggled to take care of my daughter with a man who refused to get a job and help us out. When things got really bad between us, I finally asked my mother for help. She was the one who directed me back to God. She helped me believe that God wasn't through with me and that I could be renewed in Christ.

"My favorite scripture is in the first chapter of Jude: *Now unto him that is able to keep you from falling, and to present you faultless before the presence of his glory with exceeding joy, to the only wise God our Saviour, be glory and majesty, dominion and power, both now and ever. Amen."*

"That's a powerful scripture, Sister Margie," Lamont said. "That scripture also proves my point. God is able to present us faultless, but not enough people are relying on God to keep them from falling."

"Some people have been beaten down for so long that they just don't know how to allow God to help them."

"Again," Lamont said, "I don't understand that. Are you saying that Christians aren't reading their Bibles?" Lamont lifted his thick Bible off of the desk. "Because this book has all the answers any Christian would ever need to live right. These are not just words on paper... it is the living Word."

"I agree, but, Pastor, I also think the problem runs deeper than Christians not reading the Bible." Margie moved from her spot on the couch, to the chair in front of Lamont's desk. "Earlier today Marcus left your office after telling you that he's going to go live with a man. Stephanie stormed out of here disillusioned by the thought of Christian principles, because all it got her was a down-low husband. Diane came to church all beat up and tried to accuse Deacon Benson of doing it. So, my question to you is, what are you going to do about it?"

Lamont shrugged his shoulders. "What can I do? My job as pastor is to plant and water, but God gives the increase. So, if these people don't want to live by the principles set forth in the Bible, then I have to let them go."

Shaking her head, Margie said, "And I think that very thought is what's wrong with the church today. Nobody wants to go out and get the lost anymore. We're all too concerned about looking blessed in our big homes and luxury cars, to take time out of our day to wonder why sister so-and-so or brother who-knows, doesn't come to church anymore."

"I have tried to reach out to saints that leave the church at least once after they've left," Lamont defended himself.

But Margie wasn't letting him off the hook so easily. "I don't mean any disrespect, Pastor, but I've noticed that we don't have an outreach program. No one from this church goes door to door in this neighborhood to talk to the people about their salvation or lack thereof. No one checks the membership logs to see who no longer attends the church and then attempts to find out why."

The look on Lamont's face said it all. He hadn't even contemplated doing those things. "This is a new church, Sister Margie. I only have three hundred members, so I doubt that I would even have enough mature Christians able and willing to handle the things you suggest."

"I understand how busy you are, Pastor Lamont. I only brought those things up because you asked me how I managed to stay with God even after the things I have been through. I'm just grateful that my mother was able to pray for me and help me to see that God still loves me, because if she hadn't been there, no one else would have come looking for me."

"My hope is that people will come to church so they can hear from God, instead of running from it."

Margie shifted in her seat as she asked, "Is it okay if I say what I really think?"

Lamont laughed. "You mean you've been holding back?"

Margie smiled, but said nothing.

"Go ahead, Sister Margie. What do you really think about this situation?"

"The problem with people coming to church to hear from God is that so many preachers are out there doing wrong that the people are getting confused. They don't know what is permissible for them to do, versus what they should and shouldn't be doing.

"I mean, look at that preacher who just got caught carrying on with teenage boys, and had to settle out of court with them to keep their mouths shut... and what about that handsome preacher who used to broadcast his program on The Word Network who was going out of the country meeting up with some stripper that he was dating. I can go on and on about the sin in the church that seems to start right in the pulpit."

"Okay, I'll give you that. Some of these preachers think they can do anything they want and still get behind a pulpit, but that doesn't give the members of the congregation a license to sin or to just give up on God."

Margie understood where Lamont was coming from. Before she fell into sin, she would have said the same thing. But now she knew the truth... sin begets more sin. "I don't agree with you," she stood up and walked to the door, but before she left she turned around and said, "Whether you or other pastors want to deal with the issue or not, I truly believe that people who would have otherwise come to God and then lived according to his commandments, can't do it because there is just too much sin in the pulpit."

"Sin in what pulpit?" Lamont stood to challenge her.

"I'm not talking about you, Pastor Lamont. I believe that you truly have a heart for God and want to please Him. But the church has been infested with so many who would seek to live any kind of way and then stand before God's people as if the call to live holy is just an Old Testament thing that went out the window when this New Testament grace entered the picture. And I simply don't believe that is the case."

Lamont thoroughly believed in the New Testament grace that Margie seemed to believe was just some license to sin. He just couldn't understand why grace and mercy seemed to be on vacation. He lowered his head and prayed, asking God to reveal to him what was really going on, so that he would be able to help the saints of God.

ELEVEN

Struggling to pull himself out of a deep, terrifying sleep, Lamont heard himself scream and scream some more as blood kept rising from the ground and screaming at him to do something. But Lamont just kept screaming back, "What can I do? I don't know what to do."

Lamont turned to JT and begged him, "Man, please do something to help these people."

But when JT lifted his hands to help one of the women drowning in blood, his hands were already full of blood and he could do nothing to help.

Lamont ran to the edge of the pool of blood and searched for a way in. When he could find none, he put his hands to his head and screamed for God to help the people.

Then Lamont heard a still small voice whisper to him, "Innocent blood calls to me. Who will give an account for them?"

"What can I do?" Lamont screamed again. "I don't know what to do."

Shaken, Lamont was jolted from the nightmare that had been assaulting him. He sat up in bed and as his eyes began to focus, he spotted his Bible on the nightstand. Seeking to understand what God was trying to tell him, he grabbed his Bible and prayed for direction as he opened it. His eyes landed on Deuteronomy 23:14:

For the Lord your God moves about in your camp to pro-
tect you and to deliver your enemies to you. Your camp
must be holy, so that He will not see among you anything
indecent and turn away from you.

After reading that scripture Lamont felt compelled to do a study on holiness. He turned to Isaiah 35:8: *And a highway will be there; it will be called the Way of Holiness. The unclean will not journey on it; it will be for those who walk in that Way; wicked fools will not go about on it.*

As he prayed, "Lord, show me what you want me to see," he turned to Leviticus. In chapter eleven verse forty-five he read: *I am the Lord who brought you up out of Egypt to be your God; therefore be holy, because I am holy.*

"I understand that You are holy, Lord. But what does that have to do with innocent blood calling out to You?" Lamont asked. When no answer came, he asked another. "Who am I, Lord? How am I supposed to convince Your people to live holy when this world we live in loves sin and even ridicules anyone who dares to call their lifestyle sin?"

He then turned to Leviticus 19:2 and began reading...

Speak to the entire assembly of Israel and say to them: 'Be holy because I, the LORD your God, am holy.

And continued reading down to Leviticus 20:7: *Consecrate yourselves and be holy, because I am the LORD your God.*

After reading the scriptures and communing with God, Lamont began to worry once again that he had bitten off more than he could chew. Who was he that he would be able to direct God's people to this highway of holiness that was spoken of in the book of Isaiah?

He picked up his phone and dialed JT. When he answered, Lamont said, "Man, I really hope you have time for me today, because I need to run something by you."

"I always have time for a brother in Christ. Since it's such a warm day, I was just getting ready to barbeque for Cassandra and the kids, so come on over."

Lamont shook his head as if JT could see his response. "I don't want to interfere with your family time."

"Boy, if you don't cut that stupid talk. You are family. Now get on over here," JT yelled through the phone line.

"Thanks, I'll be over in about an hour," Lamont said just before hanging up the phone. He jumped in the shower, running the water over his face as he tried to rid himself of the awful feeling the bloody nightmare brought his way. But no amount of water could cleanse his mind from the bloody images in his head.

He jumped out of the shower, threw on a sweat suit and rushed out of his house, seeming to believe that he'd be leaving the blood in his dreams behind him if he just left his house. But even as he drove to JT's house, with eyes wide open, the images kept coming.

JT was flipping burgers on the grill when Lamont stepped on the back patio. Without turning around to see who had come onto the patio, JT said, "I put a turkey leg on for you."

"Thanks man, I'm sure that your burgers are wonderful, but I don't eat no parts of a cow or a pig." Lamont came and stood next to JT. "Do you need help with anything?"

"Sanni and I have it covered. She's getting ready to bring out the baked beans and potato salad."

Lamont, his attention toward the back yard where Jerome and Aaron were laughing and playing with Lily on the swing set said, "Then I guess I'm going to play with the kids." As Lamont picked up a football that had been laying dormant in the grass, he yelled at Jerome and said, "Boy, get off that swing and come catch this ball."

"Uncle Lamont!" the three yelled in unison.

Jerome got off the swing set and said, "I was just playing with Lily. She likes me to swing with her," he said as if an eight year old needed an excuse to enjoy time spent on a swing set.

"Hey, I'm going to get on that swing next," Lamont said with laughter in his eyes. "I just wanted to throw the ball with you a little bit. I heard that you've turned into a running back while I've been building my church." Lamont threw the ball.

Jerome caught it and said, "Yeah, Dad says that I'm going pro for sure. But Mommy said I should try out for basketball or baseball."

Lamont laughed. "She just doesn't want you getting hurt, that's all."

"She treats me like a baby," Jerome complained.

"I heard that," Cassandra said as she came out onto the patio and placed the food on the table."

"I don't think you should say anything else," Lamont warned Jerome.

Jerome tossed the football to Lamont and ran back towards his brother and sister.

"Come on and eat," JT called to everyone.

The kids ran to the table and Lamont sat down with them also. As JT put the meat on the table and everybody started grabbing buns and putting potato salad and bake beans on their plate, JT said, "I have some awesome news that I want to share with everyone."

Cassandra looked up from her plate. "What's up?"

"I just received a call from the producers of the Word in Action Channel and they want to televise the last day of the revival."

Cassandra jumped up. "Oh my God, JT, that's awesome!" She hugged JT and said, "Baby, I'm so proud of you. You've been working hard to rebuild our church and now God is rewarding you."

Lamont hadn't responded; he was drifting as he gazed down at the ground.

"Um, earth to Lamont," JT said.

Lamont pulled away from his thoughts and smiled at his mentor. "That's great news, JT. I'm happy for you."

Cassandra sat back down.

JT studied Lamont for a moment. "So what's on your mind? " JT asked once the kids had eaten and were once again playing in the back yard, "You didn't sound right when you called earlier,"

After waking from that awful nightmare, all Lamont could think to do was call JT. But now that he was sitting with him and Cassandra, he felt a bit foolish... like a child running to his parents after the boogie man chased him in his dreams. Lamont shook his head. "I don't even know where to begin."

"JT said that you sounded terrified when you called," Cassandra stated as she scooped up the paper plates off of the patio table. "So what brought that on?"

"I wouldn't say I was terrified." Growing up on the rough side of New Orleans, no guy ever admitted to being terrified of anything, not unless he wanted to get beat down just on GP every day of his natural born life. Cassandra might have been like a big sister to him, but he still couldn't bring himself to admit his fear. "It was more like I was concerned about some things that God was showing me."

Cassandra threw the plates in the trash and then sat back down with JT and Lamont. JT asked, "Okay, so what's got you so concerned?"

Lamont put his head in his hands and shook it, but just as the water in his shower hadn't been able to drown out the visions in his head, this hadn't worked either. "God is speaking to me, but I just don't know what He wants from me or how I can do it." He recanted his dream, then followed up with his time in the Word as God directed him to scriptures on living holy.

JT stretched out his legs and leaned back in his seat as he

pondered the situation. "And you say that I was there and every time you looked to me for help you saw blood on my hands?"

"It was the strangest thing I've ever dreamed," Lamont admitted. "As I tried to rescue one of the victims out of the blood, I kept screaming for your help. It was odd." He frowned, "You weren't in this bloody pool, but every time you lifted your hands, blood would drip from them. Then it seemed as if you were stuck and couldn't move."

"Sounds like God is trying to reveal some deep revelation to you," Cassandra said.

"Yeah, but I honestly don't know what I can do to help." Lamont stood up and paced in front of the patio table. "I mean, I'm only one man."

JT stood next to him and put his hand on his shoulder. "John the Baptist was just one man, but he prepared the way for Jesus Christ." JT moved Lamont back to the table. When they sat down, JT was silent for a moment as he looked at his mentee with wonderment in his eyes.

JT knew something, Lamont could feel it.

"I think I was wrong about you not being ready for leadership. Maybe God has been preparing you for such a time as this."

"But I don't know what to do, JT, that's the problem."

"Don't you worry about that. Just as God has just revealed to me what your dream meant, I believe that He will show you what He wants you to do." JT then gave Lamont a stern look as he said, "You are the one Lamont. So, you do as God directed you and keep yourself consecrated before God." JT smiled as he leaned back in his chair.

"What are you smiling about all goofy like that?" Cassandra asked with a confused look on her face.

"If I revealed it to you, you probably wouldn't even believe me. Lamont probably wouldn't believe it either."

"Try us," Lamont said

JT stood up and pointed at Lamont. "You're a modern day John the Baptist... You are anointed and appointed to make the way straight for the return of Jesus, my brother."

Lamont closed his eyes as confirmation hit him. He had just tried to tell God that he wasn't a modern day Moses or John the Baptist, but now as JT stood there pointing at him, it was as if the hand of God was pointing at him and giving him an assignment. Lamont only prayed that he was up for the challenge.

Later that night as JT and Cassandra lay in bed, cuddling and watching a movie, she revisited the talk with Lamont, "You know, babe, with all the excitement of you declaring that Lamont was on an assignment from God and all, I totally forgot to ask you to clarify something else that you said earlier."

Holding onto his wife, JT brushed a soft kiss along the back of her neck as he said, "What's that, Sanni?"

She turned to face her husband. "You told Lamont that God had revealed to you the meaning of his dream. I still feel a little confused by some of it, so I was hoping that you would be able to share the revelation with me."

Pain etched across JT's face.

"What's wrong?" Sanni asked.

JT closed his eyes for a moment. When he opened them again a lone tear drifted down his cheek. "I wish I had been a better man."

"What's wrong, baby... tell me." She put her hand to his cheek to comfort him.

Sitting up in bed, he pulled Cassandra up with him. "I don't want to upset you."

"You're not upsetting me,; you're scaring me, JT. What's going on?"

"No baby, don't lose your trust in me now. I've kept my word to you these last five years. I haven't done anything contrary to the Word of God, I can promise you that. It's what I did before... that's what put the blood on my hands."

Hesitantly, Cassandra nodded, "Go on."

"Sanni, if I discuss this with you, you've got to promise not to get mad at me for past sins."

She held up her right hand. "You have my word, JT. I just want to know what's going on."

"Okay, here it is... the blood on my hands that Lamont saw has to do with all the women I cheated on you with."

As if lightening had struck, Cassandra visibly jumped.

"I don't want to get you upset," JT quickly said.

After a moment, Cassandra said, "It does hurt to think about all of that. I'm not upset. I know that's your past. Now, go on and stop trying to tiptoe around me."

"God showed me that the people Lamont saw who were bleeding and dying needed someone to help get them out of harm's way. I couldn't, because I had placed many women in harm's way when I convinced myself and them it was okay to commit fornication and adultery. I confused them to the point that they no longer knew right from wrong.

"It will take someone like Lamont who has not been spotted by sin, since he gave his life to God to help turn the people around."

"That's deep. Because if it's like that, then a whole lot of preachers need to figure out how they can get the blood off their hands," Cassandra said.

"Ain't that the truth."

They lay back down and then Cassandra asked, "Does it make you feel bad that somehow God doesn't think you are fit for the assignment that He is giving to Lamont, your mentee?"

"It hurts that I've failed God," JT admitted, but then just as quickly added, "but I'm okay with it because I know that God has forgiven me for all my dirt and that He loves me. But just like King David couldn't build God's temple because of the blood on his hands, I will step aside and allow my spiritual son to help rebuild God's house in the way He wants it built."

"And because of that forgiveness, King David will always be remembered as a man after God's own heart," Cassandra whispered and then drifted off to sleep.

TWELVE

Tony Denario was not a well man. His doctor had just informed him that his heart was beating irregularly and that two of his arteries were clogged. Yeah, yeah, yeah, he knew it was from being overweight, or rather from never saying no to fried chicken, fried fish, and fried ice cream. He'd even taken up the greasy habit of eating fried pickles. Now Doctor Cartwright was telling him that he had to lose a hundred pounds and start eating salads.

That news alone made him want to kill somebody. But the fact that he had no insurance and would need money set aside in case he had to have surgery, got his trigger finger to itching all the more. Tony had intended to turn down the contract that had just been put on this preacher's head, because the woman simply wasn't paying enough money.

If it wasn't for his poor health, Tony would have laughed at that scrimpy five thousand dollar offer for one dead preacher. But since he'd never invested in a health care plan and now needed money for an operation, he had to look out for himself. But he still didn't feel good about what he was about to do.

He put the key in the lock as he opened his mother's front door. His mother was seventy-two, with white-gray hair and a beautiful smile that always seemed to brighten Tony's day.

He would do anything for her. But this last thing she had just asked him to do was something that he wished he could say no to.

"Hey boy-o," Mrs. Denario said as her son walked into the kitchen. "I was just fixing your plate."

"How'd you know I was coming by?" Tony asked while eyeing the heaping plate of macaroni and cheese, collard greens, yams and fried chicken."

"You always come over on Sunday."

"Only because you cook all this good food." Tony took the plate from his mother, sat down and started vacuuming up the food. Once he had cleaned half the plate he said, "Now Mom, you know I really shouldn't be eating all this fattening food. My doctor says I need to take some weight off."

"That's nonsense. You don't need to lose no weight," His mom said as she sat her three hundred pound girth into the seat next to him."

"You just can't see it because I'm your son and you love me," Tony said while slurping up the collard green juice that was the only thing left on his plate.

"Who else is supposed to say good things about you, if not your mama?" She pinched her son's round cheeks.

Tony gave an aw-shucks grin as he took his plate back to the stove and filled it up again with his second helping.

When he returned to the table and sat back down, his mother asked, "So, will you be able to take me to that revival next Sunday night?"

"To tell you the truth, Mom, I really don't want to attend that revival. And I don't know why you do either."

"What's wrong with attending a revival?"

"I hear that the pastor is not such a good man."

"Well there are three pastors that are in charge of this revival, so which one are you talking about?"

Tony knew that his mother didn't like it when he spoke ill

of preachers, so he took her frown as a hint to shut up. "Okay Mom, no big deal. I'll take you."

"Hey Dynasty, I haven't heard from you in a little while so I was just calling to check on you, girl," Margie said when her friend answered the phone.

"You mean, check up on me," Dynasty snapped.

Taken aback by her friend's tone, Margie took the phone from her ear and stared at it for a moment. When she placed the phone back against her ear, she said, "What was that comment all about?"

"Oh nothing, I just know how judgmental you and your mother can be at times."

"So, because I called to see how you are doing, since I haven't heard from you in about three weeks, I'm being judgmental?" Margie was clueless as to how their conversation turned to this.

"Look Margie, there's no need for us to play this game. I know how you feel about Walt. But you need to understand that I love him and we are going to be married. So, if you can't deal with that, then I just don't see how we can continue to be friends."

"Are you serious?" Margie honestly couldn't believe this. But then she thought back to years ago when she had been dating a married preacher and thinking that all was going to be right with the world once he divorced his wife... so she actually did understand what Dynasty was going through. But she had hoped and prayed that her friend would have come to her senses by now.

"As serious as a heart attack. So, what you need to do is figure out if you are going to accept me for who I am, and stop judging me because I'm not perfect like you."

"I'm not perfect either, Dynasty. That's the reason I've said the things I have about your so-called relationship with Pastor Jenson." It galled Margie to have to call that man a pastor; he was so foul and had no business leading God's people anywhere. But like the saying goes... some were sent, and some just went. And Walt Jenson was one who had just made himself a preacher without any confirmation from the Lord, Margie was sure of it. "You know the mistake that I made, thinking that some married preacher cared about me and wanted to be with me. I just didn't want you to make the same mistake. That's all."

"Well you don't have to worry about that, because my relationship with Walt is nothing like your relationship with JT."

Margie shook her head with sadness. "I have to get to work, Dynasty, so I can't stay on this phone, but if you need anything, please call me. Okay?"

"I can tell that you don't believe me," Dynasty said, snippily. "I'll tell you what... I'm going to send you an invitation to my wedding." *Click.*

Margie bowed her head and prayed, "Lord, please help Dynasty realize that what she is doing is wrong."

"Chile, you might as well quit wasting your breath praying for that one. She don't want to be nothing but wrong," Betty said, sneaking up on Margie.

"Huh?" Margie wished she had prayed silently. "Mama, how can you say that?"

"Cause I call 'em like I seem 'em."

"Well, all I know is that plenty of people were probably saying the same thing about me, but it wasn't true at all. I was doing wrong, but I just didn't know how to do right."

"Who you trying to fool, Margie Ann, me or yourself?" Betty sat down in the seat across from her daughter and looked her square in the face. "All you ever had to do was stop fooling around with JT if you wanted to do the right thing."

Margie shook her head in shame. "But the sad part about it is, I don't know if I ever would have stopped seeing him. I thank God that he broke it off with me after I called his wife, because if he hadn't, I would have been no different from Dynasty... believing that a man who cares nothing about her will change the world for her."

"It hurts me to hear you say that, Margie."

"But it's the truth, Mama. Sometimes sin can be so addictive that something or someone has to pull you out of it, because you can't do it on your own." She stood and carried her empty plate and coffee cup to the sink. Turning around, she leaned against the counter. "I'm sorry if it shames you to know that your daughter couldn't get herself out of harm's way, but it's the truth, Mama. It's a truth that I have to live with every day. But now that I am stronger, I'm going to be there to help others as much as I can. I'm going to write my blog for people who I was once like –wounded and not strong enough to get up on my own."

Standing, Betty walked over to Margie and wrapped her arms around her. When they broke their hug, Betty said, "Sweetie, you are stronger than you think. I could never be ashamed of you, because I am so proud of who you are. And I'm sorry if what I said led you to believe otherwise."

Margie wiped a tear from her face as she said, "Thanks, Mama." She went to her computer and wrote in her blog about becoming a woman after God's heart. After that she left the house so that she would be on time for work.

Once at work and sitting behind her desk, Margie tried to rein in her emotions about her earlier conversation with Dynasty and her mother, when Pastor Jenson walked into the church. His presence ruined all of the positive energy she had been building around herself.

"Good morning, Ms. Margie. How are you doing this fine Tuesday morning?"

She caught the way he was admiring her on the sly. Almost as if he wanted her to jumped up on her desk and beg him to have his way with her. She smiled sweetly and said, "I'm doing wonderful;, mornings are my best time of day."

"Oh, and why is that?" he asked with a curious lift of an eyebrow.

Just as sweetly as before, Margie said, "Because I sleep with a good conscience, so I wake up with a smile on my face every morning." She wanted to ask, 'How about you?' but Pastor Lamont had already warned her about mistreating his guests. She just hoped her comment hit its mark and let that be that.

He stopped gazing at her as if she were an apple pie he wanted to sample and quickly asked, "Is Lamont in?"

Margie kept smiling, knowing full well, that Mr. No-good had received her message. "He certainly is. I'll ring and let him know that you're on the way to his office." With that she turned away from him, picked up the phone and dialed Lamont.

"Yes, Sister Margie."

"Pastor Jenson is here to see you. He should be at your door by now."

"Thanks for letting me know." Lamont hung up.

Margie went back to her work, but inside she was fuming that Lamont would even associate with a man like that. Her mind told her that birds of a feather flock together. But her heart told her that Lamont was not like that.

He had never stood over her desk ogling her, as Pastor Walt had just done or as JT used to. Once she calmed down, Margie thought clearly. Lamont had only treated her with respect, so, she knew that he was nothing like the man who'd just stepped into his office. Still, she wondered why Lamont was so compelled to hang around these no-good preachers.

A while later, Lamont's door opened and he and Walt stepped out. Walt slapped Lamont on the back as they passed Margie's office and said, "You're doing good for yourself. I always knew you had it in you."

Lamont said, "I thank God for each and every blessing."

"There you go being all spiritual again. Can't you just take a compliment and let that be that?" Pastor Walt asked snidely.

"I thank you for the compliment, but I still thank God for all His blessings." Lamont stopped walking, stuck out his hand for Walt to shake, and then said, "I'll see you on Sunday."

They were standing near Margie's office, so she overheard Pastor Walt say, "Will you at least consider my request?"

"I don't see what there is to consider. I don't operate like that. It seems too much like pimping God's people."

With a sneer on his face, Walt said, "Yes, I guess with all that dirty money you got from your jailbird daddy, you don't need to take up a second offering to feed your family, but my daddy wasn't no thief, so he didn't steal me a bunch of money."

Lamont turned away from Walt and began walking back to his office. He called over his shoulder, "Get out of my church, Walt."

Margie couldn't help herself, she started giggling when Lamont told Walt to get out of the church.

As Lamont passed her office, he saw her laughing and stepped into her office. "What's so funny?"

She glanced up in mid giggle. Embarrassed at having been caught listening in on his conversation, Margie stopped laughing, stood up and said, "I-I wasn't trying to—"

That started Lamont laughing. "You were eavesdropping on my conversation."

"No I wasn't."

He stepped further into her office and confronted her. "Yes, you were. And you know what? I think you like what you heard. But why would you be giddy over me throwing a preacher out of the church?"

Sheepishly, Margie made up her mind to be truthful. He certainly needed to be thrown out as far as she was concerned. "Why you are even bothering to do this revival with his slimy self, I just don't understand."

"Margie," he said in a warning tone.

"No, I'm serious, Pastor Lamont. My mother always says,

'Bad company ruins good intentions'. And look at him," she pointed in the direction Walt had taken to leave the church," over here trying to get you to get more money out of people who barely have enough to pay their bills."

"I understand what your mama says, but God says, 'What you call unholy, He calls holy." With that, Lamont turned and went to his office.

THIRTEEN

Before Diane got involved with JT and had to deal with all of the fallout after she had his baby, she had been best friends with Cynthia Jenson. Cynthia was the daughter of a bishop and came from a long line of bishops and pastors. Needless to say, she had been expected to marry a preacher herself. So, while Diane was still married to Benson, she had fixed her friend up with Walt, who at the time was a minister serving under JT.

Walt had instantly fallen in love with Cynthia and had asked her to marry him within three months after they began dating. But Cynthia had been adamant about only marrying a pastor. Once Walt had informed her that his goal was to one day have his own ministry, Cynthia quickly agreed to marry him. She then used all of her resources to help Walt obtain a church to pastor.

Diane was happy that things had worked out for her friend, but she never understood why Cynthia abandoned her at a time when she needed her the most... especially since she had helped her snag her husband. Oh, Diane knew that Walt wasn't the most faithful husband, but he paid the bills and kept her in high fashion. So as far as Diane was concerned, she had done Cynthia a favor and it was time that miss high and mighty recognized who her friends are.

Diane borrowed a cell phone from one of the inmates who was going with a guard and had managed to get him to sneak a phone in for her. She dialed Cynthia's number and waited three rings before the diva answered.

"Speak now or hold it until later," was the way the first lady of New Hope Church answered the phone.

"You know, you really need to get some home training," Diane said as she rolled her eyes.

"Diane? Is that you, girl?"

"You know it is. Too bad the call didn't come from my home number, or you could have just ignored the call as you always do."

"Whatever. Anyway, I thought you were in jail—something about being a deadbeat mom."

Cynthia thought she was so smart, but Diane had her number. "Well I'll be out in two days and I need your help to stay out."

"Help?" Cynthia said the word as if she'd never heard of the concept. "How am I supposed to help you?"

"If I can't get my child support paid, Benson is going to have me locked right back up. Two weeks is one thing, but if they lock me up again, it will be for six months or a year."

"Why don't you just pay your child support?" Cynthia asked. "I mean come on Diane, only a real loser brings a child into the world and expects someone to feed, clothe and put a roof over their head."

Diane put her hands on her hips and angrily said, "Don't act like you've never been broke. Before I hooked you up with Walt, you couldn't even pay your rent without help from your dad every month."

In a tone that indicated that she was bored with the conversation, Cynthia said, "What do you want from me, Diane?"

"I don't want anything. I need ten thousand dollars."

Cynthia laughed. "Call me back when you get serious."

"Oh, I'm serious all right. And if you had been any kind of friend, you would have already offered to help me. But you might be interested to know that I've made friends while I've been in jail. And some of them seem to have a few things to say about you. I'm sure you don't want me to repeat what I've been told, now do you?"

The line went silent.

Diane asked, "How soon can I expect the money?"

Scoffing, Cynthia asked, "How do you expect me to come up with ten thousand dollars?"

"I'm sure you'll figure it out. I'll meet up with you on Sunday at the revival," Diane said and then hung up.

But the Israelites acted unfaithfully in regard to the devoted things... So the Lord's anger burned against Israel. Lamont read as God directed him in Joshua, chapter seven.

As Lamont was reading the Bible that morning, every time he came across the word Israel or Israelite, God seemed to replace it with the word *Christians.*

While in his office, Lamont fell to his knees, with tears in his eyes. God was revealing to him why Christians weren't receiving help from God in this most dark hour. His congregation was praying for the sick, but the saints were still dying back to back and other saints were leaving the church all together. He cried out with a loud voice and bowed his head in reverence to his Lord.

His office door flew open and, looking like a wild woman ready for a fight, Margie ran in. "Are you all right, Pastor Lamont?" she asked.

"Take your shoes off and close the door. This is holy ground and I don't want anyone else to enter right now."

Margie did as he commanded, and then stood still waiting on direction for her next move.

Lamont wiped the tears from his eyes. He looked up at

Margie and said, "God has been dealing with me about some of the things you and I have talked about, and I..."

"Okay, what do you need me to do?" she asked softly.

He held out a hand to her. "Come and sit with me."

Margie obliged.

He put his Bible on the floor in between them, and then began reading again, "Christians have sinned; they have violated My covenant, which I commanded them to keep. They have stolen, they have lied... that is why the Christians cannot stand against their enemies; they turn their backs and run because they have been made liable to destruction. I will not be with you anymore unless you destroy whatever among you is devoted to destruction."

Lamont finished and glanced at Margie. They were quiet with their thoughts.

Without warning, Margie closed her eyes and began praying for him. God was trying to show him something, and Margie prayed that he would get everything he was meant to get out of the text he'd just read. "Oh Lord, My God... You are a strong tower and we know that the righteous can come to You and be healed. You are mighty and full of wisdom, so now I pray that You continue to direct Pastor Lamont in the way in which You have for him to go. Guide his heart and his mind, in Jesus name I pray. Amen."

When she finished praying, Lamont said, "JT thinks that God has given me an assignment to turn people's hearts back to Him."

Margie frowned at that. "Shouldn't every pastor have an assignment like that from God?"

"Exactly," Lamont said, smiling at the fact that she seemed to be understanding his dilemma. "Every preacher does have that assignment, but not all of them can fulfill it.

"God showed me that even though most pastors truly want to help the saints, they can't because they've done too much... got too much blood on their hands."

"So, what are you saying?" Margie asked.

"I guess I'm agreeing with you now. Remember when you told me that too much sin was going on in God's house for Him to bless us. Well, I think that you are right. And if we want to begin seeing God's healing and restoring power in the church again, then we are going to need to consecrate ourselves."

Confusion was on Margie's face. "Now, when you say, 'consecrate ourselves', what is it exactly that you want us to do?"

Lamont was just as perplexed as she was. "I'm waiting on God to give me further direction on that. I don't just want to generically ask the people to fast, when God might be requiring something else. Or He might want us to do it for a certain period of time. I'm trying to stay in my Word so that I can hear clearly from Him, because I don't want to lead the people down the wrong path."

Awestruck, Margie said, "I believe in you, Pastor Lamont. You won't lead the people astray. God will give you direction."

He stood up and lifted her off the floor, as well. They stood there staring at each other, and then Lamont became aware that not much space separated them and that his hand was still holding her arm. For one electrified moment, Lamont saw Margie in a white gown, walking down the aisle of the church toward him. He stepped back and shook his head, trying to remove the image from his mind. *What was God doing to him?*

As awestruck as she seemed a moment ago, now Margie just seemed nervous. She moved around his office, looking at the floor, the walls, the paper on his desk all as she made her way to the door. "I need to get back to work. Just let me know if you need anything else from me," she said as she put her shoes back on and left his office.

"That went well," Lamont said to himself as he realized

that while he was picturing Margie in a wedding gown, he must have been gazing at her in such a manner that must have unnerved her. "Great, now she thinks I'm just like the rest of the pastors that she has known." Lamont shook his head as he sat back down behind his desk, still trying to figure out what consecration looked like for his church.

FOURTEEN

Walt was in his favorite place. In bed with a woman who wasn't his wife. When Walt married Cynthia, he hadn't wanted to be a pastor. He'd known that God had a ministry for him and had always thought he fit best in the Helps ministry. He'd served as an armor bearer for JT and had even been given the title of minister because of the work he did with men's prisons and homeless shelters. But Cynthia wouldn't marry him unless he agreed to become a pastor. She'd said that he wasn't fully utilizing his God given abilities.

So, Walt had jumped into his newfound role as pastor with zeal and the woman of his dreams by his side. Walt would never admit it, but he'd never thought he could get a woman as gorgeous as Cynthia... not with his slight weight problem and his looks. Walt didn't fool himself, even though he wasn't bad on the eyes, he was never the most handsome guy in any room he'd ever been in. But Cynthia had wanted him anyway.

Everything had gone well for them at first, but then he started counseling some of the women in the church. Those women began telling him how lucky Cynthia was to have such a wonderful man as he was. Pretty soon, Walt found himself counseling quite a few of his women parishioners in the bed. He turned over and pulled Dynasty close to him as he said, "I'm speaking at a convention next month, and I think I'm going to take you out of town with me. Let you keep me company in my hotel room."

"What about your wife? Don't you normally take her out of town with you?"

"You let me worry about Cynthia."

Dynasty turned to face him as she asked, "Why do you even have to worry about her? Why haven't you asked her for a divorce yet?"

Walt rubbed Dynasty's back. It always came to this with the church women he dated. But Walt had a ready answer. "These things take time, baby."

"How much time?" Dynasty shot back.

"How ever much time it takes," he said with a shrug. He then grabbed Dynasty and tried to get her back under the cover with him.

Dynasty pushed Walt away and sat up in the bed. With a frustrated look on her face, she said, "I can't keep doing this, Walt."

Walt was getting sick of playing this game with his women. He sat up and said, "Now baby, don't start this stuff again."

"But you promised me that we would be together," Dynasty pouted. "I don't feel right sneaking behind your wife's back. And Margie keeps making me feel as if I'm doing something wrong."

Walt shook his head. "How many times have I told you to keep your friends out of our business? Not to mention the fact that I'm a preacher and I could lose my ministry if word got around about you and me."

"But Walt, I don't understand why you haven't asked your wife for a divorce yet. That way, things between us wouldn't have to be a secret." Smiling, Dynasty added, "We could even get married in front of the entire church. That way God would bless our union and you wouldn't have to worry about living with a woman you don't love."

Walt lifted a hand, slowing Dynasty's roll. "Now, wait a minute, I never said that I didn't love my wife. Cynthia has been there for me and she is a wonderful first lady."

Dynasty pulled herself up so that she was now sitting so close to Walt that their bare arms were rubbing against each other as she said, "If you love her so much then why are you with me?"

He gave her a 'duh' look. "Because you were down with the program. At least you had been. Now you're letting your friends convince you that what we have is wrong instead of trusting that I know what's best for us."

"I do trust you, Walt baby. I just want to be right with God and I can't do that if I keep sleeping with you without being married."

"And you think it would please God for you to bust up my marriage and leave my children to be raised in a single parent home?"

Her brows crinkled in confusion. "Are you serious, Walt?" Her hands went to her hips. "You're the one who said you wanted to marry me. When we first got together, you kept telling me that you wanted nothing more than to be with me, but now I'm a home wrecker."

He pulled Dynasty into his arms. "Come on baby, I didn't come over here to argue with you. I wanted to spend the afternoon with my baby and forget about the craziness of this world."

"I feel like a fool and like I should have listened to Margie's warnings about falling for some married man," Dynasty said, "You promised to marry me!"

He pulled her back down and as she lay next to him, cuddling in his arms, Walt said, "You know what my mama always used to tell me."

"What?"

"Good things come to those who wait. I believed her and

look how the Lord has blessed me." He kissed the back of her neck. "So, now you just need to believe in me."

"It's getting harder and harder to believe in you, Walt. Especially since you just confessed to being in love with your wife."

"I don't know, Mama, maybe you were right," Margie said after putting her daughter to bed and then coming back down to the family room to hang out with her mom.

Betty was watching Hoarders - Buried Alive and didn't respond.

"Mom, did you hear me?"

Betty turned to her daughter. "Girl, I'm sorry, I was sitting here trying to figure out how anybody could get so depressed that they just let trash build up around them until they could barely get in and out of their house." She pointed at the television. "I mean look at that."

"I said, I think you were right about my working for Pastor Lamont being a mistake."

Betty lifted her remote and turned the television off. She turned to her daughter with fury in her eyes, "Did that JT do something to you?"

"No Mama, JT hasn't come near me."

"You said he approached you a couple of months ago," Betty corrected.

"That was the first time I saw him at the church, and really all he was doing that day was trying to apologize, but I never gave him the opportunity before I lit into him."

"You did the right thing, so don't start feeling bad about that now."

Margie knew that her mother felt that everyone deserved a second chance, but preachers who messed up, only got fire and brimstone from her. "I keep praying about my animosity towards JT and I really do believe that God expects me to be able to forgive and move past all of this. I don't know what's hindering me... but I do believe that unforgiveness blocks the blessing that God is trying to send my way."

Betty shook her head. "Well, if it's not JT, what's got you so upset?"

"To tell you the truth, Mama, I don't know if I'm overreacting or not," Margie said.

"Well, tell me what's going on, maybe I can help."

Margie wasn't so sure. Sometimes her mother went a little too far with her help and her comments. But Margie really needed to talk to someone. "I'm starting to have feelings for Pastor Lamont."

Betty threw her hands up in the air. "Oh Lord Jesus, help us right now," Betty exclaimed as she jumped off the couch and paced the floor. "Girl, didn't you get enough of fooling around with these no-good preachers when JT sent you through all of that drama?"

"See, this is why I didn't want to talk to you about this. I knew that you would automatically assume that something was going on between me and Pastor Lamont."

With a look of guilt on her face, Betty sat back down. "I'm sorry. I didn't mean to jump to conclusions." She waved her hand as if giving her the floor. "Please continue."

Margie was hesitant now. "Just forget it." Margie picked up the remote and turned the television back on.

Betty took the remote from her and turned the television back off. "I'm serious, Margie. I'm ready to listen. I've watched your growth over the years, so I trust your judgment."

"Thanks for saying that, Mom."

"I mean it, Margie. I really do."

Margie put her feet up on the couch and got comfortable. "Well first of all, I think the thing that really attracts me to Lamont is his love for God. He really desires to do God's will and is not playing games at all."

"You really believe in him, huh?"

"I do, Mom. These last few months of working for him, has shown me just what kind of man he is. And I can tell that he really cares about the people God has entrusted to him."

"So are you telling me that the fact that this boy is gorgeous has nothing to do with what you're feeling for him?" Betty asked, the skepticism heavy in her tone.

"I didn't say that," Margie grinned. "I'm not blind and Pastor Lamont is definitely easy on the eyes."

"Easy on the eyes?" Betty slapped her knee as she said, "That man is eye candy with a sugary sweet peppermint on top. When I attended your church last weekend, I could barely read my Bible for watching him."

"Mom," Margie playfully nudged her mother. "You're not supposed to notice things like that."

"Girl please, I might be older than you, but I'm not dead yet."

They giggled. Then Margie said, "Okay Mom, you're right about how handsome he is, but I'm telling you, it's not just that. He has this presence about him, like if it ain't about Jesus then don't even bother him with the discussion. And I like that about him."

Betty said, "Yeah, especially since so many of these slick preachers think they are getting away with their dirty, but it seems as if God has stamped a scarlet letter on their forehead." She shook her head. "Oh they think they are fooling all of us poor dumb saints, but their aura speaks of the sins they have committed.

"I wish someone would tell them that we can see sin all over them. Then maybe they'd stop getting in the pulpit and trying to preach, when they need to be somewhere repenting." As Margie said these words, she realized that she no longer saw that aura of sin around JT, he, in fact, had the same presence about him as Lamont. She grabbed her mother's arm and said, "Oh my goodness, I owe JT an apology."

"What?" her mother exclaimed.

"It's just like you said, Mama, when a preacher is in sin, they have that slick used car salesman look about them. They don't see it, but I think God opens the rest of our eyes to it."

"Yeah, and?" Betty questioned, still not understanding what that had to do with an apology to JT.

"JT doesn't have that look anymore. He's telling the truth, Mama. He is a changed man. He's God's man and we both have to respect that."

Betty sat there for a moment, twisted her lip, and then she nodded. "Okay, let me pray on this a while. But I do agree that he who the son has set free is free indeed. So, I'll to keep my mouth shut about him, huh?"

"You and me, both," Margie said as she leaned back against the couch and said, "Now I see why Cassandra had no problem with me coming to work for the church. She believes in her husband... and if my thought process is right on this, I think she can see that I'm not trying to do wrong anymore either."

"Well, I'm glad for Cassandra. She's a good woman and she deserves a good man." Betty grabbed hold of Margie's pretty face and looked directly in her eyes as she declared, "You're a good woman also, Margie. And you deserve some happiness... I believe God has a good man out there for you. I'm not saying it's Pastor Lamont, but if it happens to be him, well then I'm all for it."

"Yeah, but Mom, how do I know if this is God, or if I'm just lusting after another man of God?"

"Pray, baby. And don't move on nothing until God reveals the truth to you."

FIFTEEN

Taking a deep breath, Margie punched in the number and prayed. "Hi Cassandra, this is Margie Milner." Margie held her breath. The last time she'd called Cassandra had been several years ago. And in Margie's confused mind at the time, she'd told Cassandra that JT was cheating on both of them. She now fully realized that the only person JT was cheating on was Cassandra and she just happened to be one of the women he was cheating with.

"Hey Margie, is Lamont treating you okay over there?" Cassandra asked good naturedly as if they were mutual friends.

It seemed as if Cassandra had no fear at all about why Margie would be calling her house. This woman had completely put her trust in her husband... as if she had unmovable faith... the kind Margie would love to have. "I wanted to call and finally thank you for your part in getting me this job."

"That's not necessary," Cassandra said.

Margie shook her head. "I disagree. The day I saw you in this office, I treated you to a full dose of suspicion and mistrust. It was uncalled for and I'm sorry."

Cassandra laughed. "You were a bit rude," she agreed.

"Yes, I was, and I have no excuse for myself, except it was the actions of my guilty conscience. I expected you to do what I probably would have done to you if the roles were reversed."

"Well then, I accept your apology."

"Thank you," Margie said and then to curb her curiosity, she asked, "Can I ask you a question?"

"Sure, what's on your mind?"

"You seem so free of bitterness. And based on what happened between us, I tend to believe that God would forgive you a little bitterness."

Cassandra laughed again. "To tell you the truth, Margie, I used to think that God should be okay with my bitterness or the reasons I had for not trusting or forgiving my husband. But then one day, I took the time to have a talk with Jesus, and He made it all better... God took the bitterness out of my heart, and I don't ever want to go back to the way I used to feel."

"You are a powerful woman of God, Cassandra Thomas."

"And so are you, Margie. You just have to remember, that where you are weak, God is strong enough to get you through whatever it is you're going through."

"Thanks Cassandra, I'll keep that in mind." They hung up and Margie got back to work.

But her conversation with Cassandra kept repeating over and over in her head as she worked her way through her assignment. Bitterness was not something that she wanted in her life. As she worked on the Sunday bulletin which held information about the weekly programs at the church and the names of the sick and shut-in, Margie noticed that the sick and shut-in list was getting longer. She kept praying for the people on the list, but lately Margie was wondering if her prayers were even reaching heaven, because the saints just didn't seem to be getting any better.

So, when JT walked into the church and went directly to Lamont's office, being careful to avoid her desk all together, as he had since the day Margie chewed him out, Margie decided that this was going to be the last day that JT would feel as if he had to sneak into his friend's church. She continued to work, and waited until Lamont and JT walked out of Lamont's office.

Lamont stopped by her desk and said, "I'm heading over to the park to view the site for this weekend's revival, but if you need to reach me, I'll have my cell phone with me."

"Okay," she said and then turned to JT and asked, "Do you think I could speak with you for a moment before you and Pastor Lamont leave?"

JT looked back at Lamont and with a worried look on his face, said, "Yeah, sure, what can I help you with?"

Lamont turned to walk away.

But Margie stopped him. "You don't have to leave, Pastor Lamont, this won't take but a minute."

Lamont pivoted on his heels, but didn't move from his spot by the door.

Taking a deep breath, Margie held JT's stare and began, "I just wanted to tell you that I believe that you are a changed man. And I wanted to apologize for the way I treated you when I first started working here."

The shock on JT's face would have been comical if Margie wasn't so serious. Recovering, he nodded. "I appreciate you saying that, Margie. And I want to let you know that I am truly sorry for what I did to you. It wasn't right and I will have to answer to God for that."

Nodding, Margie said, "And He is the only one you have to answer to. I forgive you." Margie stuck her hand out and JT shook it. She then sat back down behind her desk and got back to work as if forgiving people who brought hurt and pain into her life was something she did every day.

Tony parked his car in the circle lot adjacent to Upper Edgewater Park because this spot provided the best view of downtown Cleveland. When he was a teenager, he used to drive up there and look down at the city with dream filled eyes. At that time Tony was the star quarterback for his high school football team. He had big dreams of going to the NFL, making a name for himself and then coming back home, buying up some of that downtown real estate and being set for life. But then an injury during his freshmen year of college sent him back home to the hood.

Tony hadn't picked his current line of work. It had picked him. After coming home with no money in his pocket and no food in the cabinets at his mom's home, he had to find a way to support himself and his mother. Now that he was eighteen, she no longer received any type of assistance from the government. Her minimum wage job didn't do much past paying the rent and electric bill. Since he had been a football player, he'd always had some bulk on him, so he applied for security and body guard jobs.

The only person willing to give him a chance had been Daryl Junior, an old school gangster who had polluted the hood with heroine and crack for twenty years. Tony became his body guard and served him faithfully, taking care of problems as they came up. Through the three years of employment with Daryl, Tony had been ordered to kill eleven hustlers who'd gotten too big to remain in the same city with Daryl and his ego. When the Feds finally took Daryl down, Tony went freelance.

He got out of his car, took a small shovel out of his trunk and slow walked to the restrooms over by the pavilion area. He kept the shovel against his arm as if it were an extension of himself... nothing to see here, just strolling through the park.

When he reached the men's restroom, he quickly dug a small hole and shoved the dirt to the side. Once that was complete, he took the small shovel and placed it in the women's restroom. His client had requested that he take the preacher out during the revival, so Tony was making preparations.

After disposing of the shovel, he slow walked, while he

whistled, down to the lower level of Edgewater Park, headed for the picnic shelter. On his way to the shelter, Tony watched as three of Cleveland's finest preachers came toward him. One of them was a dead man walking, but just didn't know it.

As he came upon them, Tony nodded. Walt Jenson was on his cell phone, so he paid him no mind, Lamont Stevens nodded back, but JT Thomas stopped and shook his hand.

"Hey, don't I know you from somewhere?" JT asked

With a plastered smile on his face, Tony said, "I've brought my mother to your church a few times. She really enjoys it."

"Well, I hope to see you and your mom back real soon."

Enjoying the game, Tony said, "She asked me to bring her to the revival that you're putting on out here this weekend. So, we'll see you then."

Walt ended the call and then turned back to Lamont and JT and said, "What's the hold up? Are we going to look at this place or not?"

Lamont said, "Come on, since you're in such a hurry, let me get you on up there."

As Lamont and Walt walked off, JT said, "See you this weekend. God bless."

"Yeah," Tony said to himself as he walked away, "Hopefully, God will bless you also."

As Tony entered the picnic shelter he scanned the area for his client. She had asked that they meet here so Tony could get a feel for the area in which she'd like to have a preacher slain. He would have handled the job a few minutes ago, but Tony hadn't received payment yet, and he didn't do pro-bono jobs. The shelter was empty when he arrived. Tony sat down and waited a few minutes. After about five minutes, he figured he'd been stood up. It happens sometimes... people think they want someone dead, but when faced with making it happen, their moral code just won't allow them to go through with it. Tony didn't have a moral code, so it didn't bother him. As far as he was concerned, he was just creating more space for others to dwell on the earth.

Getting up, Tony was about to head back to his car when a woman in a navy blue jogging suit strolled into the shelter. She had a hood over her head and looked as if she was trying to hide. He flopped down and waited for her to take her seat next to him.

"Hey," she said when she sat down.

Tony wasn't much for small talk. "Did you bring my money?"

"Half, right?" She handed him a white envelope.

"I don't want to meet with you after the deed is done, so I'm going to need the other half the morning of the revival." He quickly counted the money and then asked, "You do still want the hit at the revival right?"

She hesitated for a moment. Tony said, "Hey, if you're having second thoughts, let me know right now."

She shook her head. "No, no. This needs to be done."

"Okay then, you've got two days to come up with the rest of my money." He stood up and told her, "Take my advice and don't go up by the pavilion area."

"Why?" His client nervously looked around.

"The three of them are up there checking the place out. My mark, however, doesn't realize that this is the last place he will ever see."

SIXTEEN

Lamont was on his knees again, crying out to God. Today he was praying for his fellow preachers, those who live according to God's will. He prayed that they would find the strength to continue fighting the good fight of faith and so they could teach others to do the same.

He then changed his focus and cried out to God on behalf of preachers who had gone astray. From listening to JT, Lamont learned about the torture and guilt that a man of God who chose to do the wrong thing faced on a daily basis... that is until he finally stopped being pricked by the word of God. Lamont prayed that thousands and thousands of preachers would be turned back towards God, before they went too far to be restored.

Lastly, Lamont petitioned God for himself. He admitted to the Lord that he had feelings for Margie, but that he was scared of those feelings because of what happened to his ex girl, Sonya. They had been in love with each other, and that had been why Sonya had felt so comfortable with getting on his motorcycle with no helmet.

Lamont knew now that he had been careless with another person's life, and he never wanted to feel the deep despair that came over him every time he thought of how carelessly Sonya had died again. He couldn't live with himself if being around him caused another woman's demise. And the way that Margie tackled Diane Benson at that wedding, really freaked Lamont out. Was Margie the type to run towards trouble? "God, please help me and direct me concerning my feelings for this woman."

When he was finished praying, he got off the floor, dusting off his pants. Grabbing his keys, Lamont headed out of his office.

As he was walking past Margie's desk, through the cracked door, she called after him. "Wait a minute, Lamont." She covered her mouth with her hand and then spoke again. "I mean, Pastor."

Lamont walked into her office. "It's all right, Sis. Margie. You don't have to be so formal with me all the time. I know that I'm a pastor, but my name is Lamont."

She picked up a water bottle and handed it to him. "Don't leave without this."

Lamont laughed.

"I'm serious," Margie told him. "You've been fasting all week."

He raised a questioning brow.

"You don't have to tell me that you're fasting. I work here and I know that you haven't been eating. Are you able to drink water on your fast?

He nodded.

She pushed the bottle toward him again. "I don't want you to get dehydrated, so drink."

Lamont saluted. "Yes, ma'am." He opened the bottle, took a drink and then said, "I'm headed to JT's church for our final meeting concerning the revival."

"All right, just take the bottle with you, finish drinking it and then refill it when you get to Pastor JT's church."

He laughed again and gave her another mock salute before he went on his way.

As Walt grabbed his keys to leave for his meeting with JT and Lamont his cell phone rang. He didn't recognize the number, so he started not to answer it, but then he changed his mind, sat down and answered the call. "Pastor Walt speaking."

"Where is my money?" the woman on the other end asked.

"Look, I keep telling you that I don't have any money. People have been leaving the church and tithing is way down."

"Tithing will go down even further if I tell your congregation everything I know about your old tired behind," The woman said with a sneer.

Walt regretted the day that he ever even thought about hooking up with this woman. He had been speaking at a church conference in Houston, TX, thinking that he was far enough away from home to have a little fun without anyone finding out. Walt gleefully took her hotel room key and spent the night with her. However, he never expected that she would tape the whole escapade. But she had and for the last two years, he had been her unwilling sugar daddy. "I don't have any more money, Carmen, you've taken everything from me already."

"Well, you better find a bit more or wifey pooh will be getting the shock of her life. Or maybe I'll send it to Dynasty, your new woman."

"Do what you have to do. I don't have any more money." He hung up, shaking his head as he walked out of his office. Victoria, his secretary was sitting at her desk, watching him as he walked toward her. He could see by her expression that she was about to get something started, and he really didn't have the patience for it, so instead of stopping by her desk to tell her where he was going, he kept walking.

Victoria got up and followed him to the door. She grabbed his arm as he tried to leave. "Walt, I really need to talk to you."

"This is not a good time, Victoria."

"But I haven't seen you in a month," she whined.

Lifting his eyes heavenward, as if he needed the Lord's help, Walt said, "You see me every day at work."

"You know what I mean." Victoria leaned in and whispered, "You haven't come to my house in a month."

He pushed her back and said, "Look, Victoria, I'm on my way to a meeting, but I don't think my wife would appreciate you inviting me to your home." With that he walked out of the church and headed to his meeting about the revival he was helping to host this weekend.

"Okay, are we all right with the schedule?" JT asked as he sat down at the round table in the conference room at his three thousand seat church.

"Yeah, I have a question," Walt said, while looking at the paper as if it offended him. "Why am I preaching on Friday night, while Lamont gets to preach on Saturday night? I mean, come on," Walt pointed at Lamont and said, "I know that you have three thousand members, so I understand why you're preaching the Sunday morning message, but I have fifteen hundred, Lamont only has three hundred."

"So, you think because your numbers are higher that you should get Saturday, rather than Friday?" JT asked.

"Darn straight, I do." Walt leaned back in his chair.

Lamont started silently praying. He reminded himself that he was in consecration mode, and this was not a battle worth fighting.

JT said, "Didn't you tell us that you weren't even inviting your church members to this revival?"

"You know that the people in my church are always start-ing some mess. I can't take them nowhere without shame and embarrassment."

"Don't you think that as their leader, you need to show them how not to be messy, shameful and embarrassing? Or are you telling us that you are just as messy?" Fast or no fast,

Lamont couldn't help himself. As far as he was concerned, that question needed to be asked.

"Come back and see me in a few years, after your congregation sings your praises after each sermon you preach and tell me if you aren't a little messy after that," Walt said with smugness... like he'd seen it happen to a hundred or more preachers and Lamont would be no different.

Lamont wanted to tell him that he would never be that guy. He could look Walt up in ten or even twenty years and his name would still not be as run down as Walt's was. But Lamont was gently reminded about the Bible verse that warned believers to be careful when they think they stand, lest they fall. So, he said, "My prayer is to continue to serve God without blemish."

Walt laughed.

JT said, "Back to business." JT looked down at the program schedule in front of him and said, "We have the offering scheduled right after praise and worship, but we can move it to the end of the service."

"Uh-uh. Bad idea. If you wait until the end of service, half the congregation will have already tipped out. Especially on Saturday night when Lamont is up there boring everybody with his long messages." Walt looked over at Lamont with an apologetic half smile and added, "I'm just saying."

Ignoring Walt's rude comment, Lamont said, "Why don't we just keep the offering after praise and worship."

Walt leaned forward. "Speaking of offering time... have either of you thought anymore about adding a special offering? We can get a couple of hundred dollar lines going." Walt raised his hand as if in praise to the Lord. "It will be glorious."

In unison, Lamont and JT said, "No!"

Walt held up a hand. "Hold up, brethren. Why so hostile?"

"We keep telling you that this revival is about the people of God. It's not about us fattening our pockets."

"Whatever," Walt said. Then his cell phone rang. He looked

at the number displayed, grinned and then put his cell back on his hip clip. He turned back to Lamont and JT. "If there's nothing else we need to go over, I need to be somewhere."

When he walked out of the conference room, Lamont said, "You know that was some woman ringing his phone, right?"

JT nodded. "Yeah, I know."

Lamont sat silent for a moment, then as if something had jumped into him, he got up and said, "Once again I need to ask, why in the world we have to partner with someone like him?" he jerked as if a bug had fallen on him and he was trying to shake it off.

JT didn't answer.

"Can't you see that he's no good?" Lamont tried again.

"I can see it," JT said with his head bowed as if he was in prayer.

Lamont was still standing, pacing the floor now. "Then I don't get it, JT. Why are we putting up with Walt's nonsense when we need to be worrying about souls that need to be saved?"

"Walt has a soul, too."

Lamont sighed and then sat back down. He looked at his friend and mentor. "I know that Walt is some kind of mission for you. But I can't go on this journey with you again. The man's name is so run down on the street that the people laugh at his members when they admit to attending his church."

"I understand that, too."

SEVENTEEN

At about five in the evening on Friday, Tony Denario picked up his final payment for the job he had to do that night, he then drove to Edgewater Park. Tony took a compressed duffel bag out of the trunk of his car and walked over to the restroom area. He had dug a small hole two days before, and now he was back to fill it. It wouldn't have been the smartest thing for him to walk through the park with a shovel and a duffel bag all on the same day, no matter how small the shovel or duffel. Someone might have noticed and got suspicious enough to alert the authorities. But today he just looked like a regular guy holding a duffel bag.

He reached the spot where he'd dug his small hole, and looked around. He could see no one for miles. Tony turned back around and quickly dropped the bag in the hole. He then slightly covered it with some of the dirt he had moved to the side the day before. While the revival was going on tonight, Tony would sneak off to the restroom, grab his duffel, decompress it and take out his change of clothes and his mask and then he'd shoot his target, run back to his SUV, where his duffel would be stashed, and change back into his regular clothes.

He looked at his watch as he made his way back to his SUV. His mom had asked him to pick her up at six. She wanted to arrive at the park a little early in hopes of getting a good seat.

"What Mama wants, Mama gets," Tony said to himself as he got in his SUV and sped towards his mother's house.

Margie arrived at the site at about 6:15. Lamont would not be preaching tonight, but since he was one of the planners for this revival, she wanted to make sure that everything was set for the start of the event. The park officials had placed the podium on the stage. There were three rows of chairs behind the podium for the preachers and their wives and for special guests. Margie placed several water bottles on the table that separated Lamont's chair from JT's and Cassandra's chairs. As she stood there for a moment, she noticed that Lamont was the only one who didn't have a second seat next to his. And she wondered, not for the first time, why a man as handsome and dynamic and as godly as Lamont Stevens didn't have a wife to call his own. She knew she was flirting with danger to even think about such a thing, especially with her past. Margie closed her eyes and recited, "Who the Son sets free is free indeed." Lately she had been reminding herself of this fact on a daily basis, sometimes twice a day. She had no past where Christ was concerned. She belonged to God and He belonged to her... the rest would take care of itself by and by.

A commotion in the back of the pavilion caused her to turn around. She looked past the hundreds of chairs that had been put out for the congregation, and watched as a camera crew began setting up their equipment. Lamont had told her that The Word in Action Network would be filming on Sunday when JT preached, but she had no idea that any other station was scheduled to film. She walked to the back of the pavilion to speak with the cameramen.

When she approached the tall, lanky one, Margie stuck out her hand and said, "Hello, I'm Margie Milner, I'm Pastor Steven's office manager."

"Good to meet you, Ms. Milner," he said while shaking her hand. He pointed at the cornrow wearing man standing next to him and said, "We're the camera crew. We freelance for the Word in Action Network among others."

With a look of confusion she said, "But I didn't think The Word in Action would be filming until Sunday."

"That's correct," the cameraman said, "but we'll be here tonight and tomorrow night to get some footage that we might be able to add with the Sunday event."

Margie smiled. All that fasting and praying Lamont had been doing was paying off already. For she truly believed that the exposure he was about to receive from this weekend would help to grow the church ten fold.

JT's and Walt's assistants pulled up at the same time. Margie went out to the parking area to greet them and to let them know where everything was. Walt's assistant would want to test the mic since Walt would be preaching tonight.

Diane stood on the porch of JT and Cassandra's home banging on the glass panel door as if she was getting paid to stress test the glass. "I know y'all hear me out here, so come open this door!" she yelled as she kept banging on the glass.

Cassandra swung the door open and screamed at her. "What is wrong with you, Diane? Why do you have to act as if you don't have any kind of sense every time you come over here?"

"Why did it take you so long to answer the door? Next time, answer as soon as I ring the doorbell and you won't get no drama out of me," Diane said as she stepped past Cassandra and walked into the house as if she was first lady of the joint.

As Diane put her hand on the banister preparing to trot herself up the stairs, Cassandra stopped her. "Where do you think you're going?"

"To see *my* daughter." Diane put an emphasis on the word my.

"You'll have to wait downstairs in the family room. And you'll only be able to see her for a moment because we are on our way somewhere."

Diane swung around and got in Cassandra's face. "I am so tired of you and JT thinking that you can tell me when and where I can see my own child."

"We didn't tell you anything," Cassandra corrected, while not backing down. "The courts gave you two weeks a month. And this is not your weekend for visitation, so I don't have to make any accommodations for you at all. But I'm willing to let you see Lily for a moment, provided you don't upset her."

"Don't act like you're doing me any favors. You're just jealous because your little girl died, so you want to steal my baby and try to pass her off as your own."

Cassandra's face went stone white. The death of her newborn baby girl had been one of the hardest things for her and JT to get through. It almost destroyed their marriage and their relationship with God, and now this evil woman had the nerve to stand in her home and throw it in her face. Those were fighting words and Cassandra was about to slap the taste out of her mouth.

"What's wrong? Cat got your tongue?" Diane asked with hands on hips, spoiling for a fight.

Cassandra's hand was itching to slap this woman. But at the same time it was itching, she was silently praying for strength to endure yet another Diane Benson assault. She didn't know how many more times she could turn the other cheek. But Cassandra dearly wanted to please God in all aspects of her life.

JT thundered down the stairs. His arm was outstretched as he angrily pointed toward the front door. "Get out of here, Diane. And don't you ever come back to our house again. How dare you come in here and insult my wife like that."

Diane put her hands on her hips, in protest. "I'll leave after I've seen my daughter."

"You'll leave now unless you want me to call the police." JT gave her a stern look. "We know that you just got out of jail for not paying your child support. I hope you don't want to rush back for disturbing the peace or on harassment charges."

She rolled her eyes, tossed her hair and then headed to the door. But before she left, she turned back to JT and said, "You're going to get yours for the way you messed over me. Just wait... you're going to get yours and I can't wait to see it," she said as she slammed the door behind her.

"That woman has a personality defect," Cassandra said as she shook her head. "As much as it pains me to do it, I'm going to have to pray for her tonight."

"I'm sorry," JT said, with his head bowed low.

"You should be," she said as she punched his shoulder. But then she lifted his chin with her finger and kissed him on the forehead. "But I forgive you." She then left him standing there as she went upstairs to finish getting their children ready for the revival.

EIGHTEEN

P raise and worship had already started by the time Tony helped his mother to a back row seat. The place was packed and he was truly sorry that he hadn't made it there early enough to get her the front row seating as she desired. "I'm sorry about this, Mama. I had no idea there was an accident on the highway, or I would have come the street way to get you."

His mom turned, looked at him with the joy of a mother who felt she'd raised a good boy. "You did the best you could, Tony. Don't beat yourself up about this. Our seats are fine. And we'll get even better seats tomorrow."

He wished his mother hadn't been so adamant about coming to this revival. And he wished he could tell her that the revival would go on tomorrow night, even though one of the preachers would be dead, but he had no guarantees of that.

The choir was singing *How Great is Our God* as the congregation joined in. Margie had her hands lifted high in praise to her almighty God. Margie twirled around as she continued singing praises unto God. That's when she saw Diane Benson in the back row, sitting next to a heavyset guy and an older woman. Margie's conversation with Diane flashed through her mind...when Diane asked her to give her information on JT, specifically wanting to know about his schedule.

Margie danced her way to the back of the pavilion and slid in next to Diane just as she had done at Benson and Joy's wedding. She leaned close to Diane and said, "Don't start nothing in here. This may not be a church, but God is still present."

Diane smirked as she said, "Come to knock me down again?"

"Don't start none, won't be none." Margie told her. She hoped that she would not have to rumble during this revival, but to save another saint's life, she was prepared to do whatever she had to do. The last thing Margie ever wanted to do was to sit idly by and watch another murder suicide.

"I can't believe that you are taking up for JT," Diane snapped. "You need to mind your own business, because you don't know how he and Cassandra treat me."

"There's a time and a place to handle your disagreements, but this is not it." The choir started another praise song as Margie walked away from Diane.

On her way back to her seat, Margie saw Cassandra handing off her children to one of the church assistants. She rushed over to her and said, "I need to speak with you for a moment."

Cassandra gave her a questioning glance.

"It's really important," Margie said, hoping that Cassandra wouldn't think that she was trying to start some drama and just ignore her.

Cassandra nodded and then walked off to the side with Margie. "What's going on?"

Getting right to the point, Margie said, "I don't want to alarm you, but Diane is here."

Cassandra frowned a bit. "I mean, she's annoying, but why would that alarm me?"

Margie whispered, "She asked me to keep an eye on JT while she was in jail."

"You've been spying on my husband?" Caught off guard, Cassandra responded with anger.

Margie shook her head. "Of course not. When God restored me, He completely restored me. I'm only telling you this because whenever Diane shows up in a church setting, there is drama." Margie sighed. "I just think you and Pastor JT need to keep an eye on her and be careful."

"Sorry about jumping to conclusions." Cassandra seemed to relax. "Thank you for giving me the heads up." She headed toward her seat on the stage.

Feeling as if she had done all she could, Margie returned to her seat and continued with praise and worship. Plus a whole lot of watching and praying.

"I'm worried, JT, I don't think you should do the offering tonight," Cassandra said as she sat next to her husband on the stage behind the podium.

The praise and worship music was winding down. JT looked at his wife and said, "Baby, what's wrong?"

"I don't have a good feeling about this. Margie saw Diane in the audience and she's up to something."

"We can't let Diane run our lives." He patted her hand. "God will protect us, Sanni, I promise you that. Do you trust me?"

She nodded.

Then he asked, "Do you trust God?"

She nodded again.

He stood up, kissed her hand and then said, "Let me go take care of this offering and then I'll come back over here and give you a real kiss."

"You better not come back here acting crazy. We might be at a park, but we're still at church."

JT winked at his wife and then went to the podium. He smiled at the many who had gathered for the revival and said, "Truly it is a blessing for us to gather at this park, with the lovely view of the lake surrounding us. I am standing for the offering, because my Bible tells me that it is more blessed to give than to receive..."

As praise and worship ended and JT stood behind the podium, Tony, leaned over to his mother and said, "I'm not feeling so good. I'm going to go to the restroom for a while. If my stomach doesn't stop bubbling, then I'll just sit in my car and wait for you once service is over."

Tony's mom put her hand on his shoulder. "Maybe you need to go to the hospital. You haven't been looking so good lately."

"I'll be all right, Mama. Don't worry so much about me." He walked off. And just as he'd told his mother, Tony went to the bathroom. But before going in, he stepped around to the back, reached down and pulled his compressed duffel bag out of the ground. His mom had bought this thing for him off of HSN, the home shopping network. When she gave it to him as a present, Tony knew exactly what he could use it for.

He stepped into the bathroom and decompressed the duffel bag and voilà, the bag expanded revealing a plastic Kroger bag, his navy blue sweat suit, no name brand white gym shoes, ball cap and Dick Cheney mask. He liked VP Cheney, that dude was cuckoo for Cocoa Puffs and didn't care who knew it.

Tony hurriedly put his clothes and mask on. Tony then shoved his gun into the deep pockets of his sweat pants. He then put the clothes he had changed out of into the duffel, compressed it again and then put it inside of a Kroger bag. It wouldn't do to have his duffel bag spotted. Tony would hate to have to get rid of a present from his mother. He walked out of the restroom on his way back to the pavilion.

After the offering, the choir sang one more selection and then Walt grabbed his Bible and headed for the podium. He placed his Bible in front of him, said a quick prayer and then he said, "I want to thank everyone who gave in the offering. As you all know, it takes a lot to pull together something as spectacular as all of this is." He hesitated for a moment, and then said, "So, that is why I'm going to take a moment before I bring the Word, to allow for a special offering. How many of you know that the Lord sends out his blessings to those who give to his ministries?"

Hands went up all over the pavilion.

Lamont turned to JT and whispered, "What is he doing?"

JT shook his head. "I don't know."

"He is out of control. I'm going to stop him," Lamont said as he began to stand up.

But JT lifted a hand, halting Lamont. "We'll deal with him later."

"Come on saints of God," Walt encouraged the crowd. "Stand up on your feet and dig deep in your pockets for God." He took a twenty out of his wallet and threw it in the basket. "I'll even be the first partaker of this special offering." People began walking down the aisle, putting their money in the basket. Walt turned to the choir and signaled for them to sing something so he could keep the emotions running high. "That's right," he said as more people came to the basket, "Like Pastor JT said, it's more blessed to give than to receive."

Walt was having a good time, watching the people of God march down to the front of the pavilion with money held high, willing to give for the work of the ministry. He just prayed it would be enough to pay his stinkin' blackmailer, so he could continue living his charmed life. But then he heard someone yelling. He looked down from the stage and saw Dynasty with tears running down her face.

"How dare you cheat on me!" Dynasty screamed.

Stunned at seeing his girlfriend standing in front of the stage screaming at him, he recovered quickly. Walt bent down and tried to whisper, "Go sit down, Dynasty. I'll talk to you later." He shooed her away with his hand.

But she wouldn't be moved. The tears kept coming as she said, "I saw your porno."

"Go sit down," he screamed as he looked back at Cynthia, who was seething.

"You lied to me. You lied to me," she said over and over, and then pulled a gun out of her purse and shot him.

Margie had taken off down the aisle the moment Dynasty began screaming at Walt. The shot occurred before she could get to him, but then Dynasty put the gun to her head. And Margie kept running and screaming at her friend. Begging her not to do it. How many times would she have to witness destruction in the church? When would the people simply decide to live right?

She reached Dynasty before she had a chance to pull the trigger again, grabbed her arm and pushed her down to the ground.

The cameramen looked at each other and said in unison, "We're going to be rich."

"I am so glad we came two days early. Let's put part of this online and charge for the rest of it," one of the cameramen suggested.

While the cameramen were high-fiving each other, Tony stood not far away, viewing all of the chaos that had unfolded. His mother had her hand over her mouth as if she were in shock. Backing out of the pavilion, he went back to the restroom and changed into his church clothes.

"Mom, what happened?" he asked when he came back into the pavilion.

"Tony, good Lord, where have you been?"

"I was in the restroom. What happened?" he asked again.

She pointed toward the stage. "Some woman shot Pastor Walt."

He grabbed his mother's hand. "Come on, let's get out of here."

"Mm, mm, mm, what is this world coming to?" Tony's mother asked as they made their way to his car.

NINETEEN

Walt lay on the ground moaning for help. Cynthia jumped from her seat and ran to her husband. "Oh my God, somebody help us," Cynthia screamed as she held onto Walt for dear life. Victoria, Walt's office manager ran onto the stage and pulled Cynthia off of Walt and began holding him herself.

Lamont pulled Victoria off of Walt, so Cynthia could be near her husband. He sat Victoria in one of the chairs on the stage and said, "We're going to let his wife take care of him now, all right?"

Victoria nodded and then burst out in tears.

JT dialed 911, then he grabbed the mic and said, "Come on saints, don't just stand there looking and doing nothing to help... pray for our brother," he pointed to Walt as he continued to moan on the floor. And then at Dynasty as Margie held the woman in her arms as she cried from some deep inner wound. "and our sister in Christ. They both need the Lord's help right now." Walt had either caused this woman to snap or she already had emotional problems that aided in her destruction, just like the young woman he had used and tried to toss aside. Cassandra had gotten hurt because of his misdeeds. JT would never forgive himself for that. He was just thankful that Dynasty hadn't decided to shoot Cynthia in order to get Walt free and clear of his wife. "Lord, help us all," JT said into the microphone as the saints kept praying.

The police and the paramedics arrived at the same time. Dynasty was put in the back of the police car, kicking and screaming as she declared that she had to ride to the hospital with her man. Walt hadn't heard a word that Dynasty uttered because he had blacked out by the time he had been put in the ambulance. Cynthia followed behind the paramedics, looking as if her world was being shattered into so many pieces that she would never be able to piece it back together.

JT told Cassandra to take the children home. He then told Lamont that he was going to the hospital with Walt.

"W-what do you want me to do? Maybe we should just send them all home. I'm not sure if I'm prepared to handle this on my own," Lamont said nervously as he looked out at the sea of people.

JT glanced in the direction where Lamont was looking. Some of the people were earnestly praying, some were confused, some had a look of hopelessness on their faces. He turned back to Lamont. "You're prepared. Just tell the people what God has been showing you. I can't imagine a better time to get the people's minds focused on consecration and living holy, can you?"

Finding the courage to do God's will, Lamont said, "Okay JT, you go with Walt. I've got this."

JT slapped Lamont on the back, and gave him an at-a-boy smile. "That's the man of God that I know. You're ready."

As he was walking away, Lamont tapped him on the shoulder. With sorrow filled eyes, Lamont said, "I know that I have a lot to say against Walt, but I never imagined that something like this would happen. I'll be praying for him."

"Keep him lifted, God is a wonder worker." JT was talking about a God that he knew that he knew, and nothing could make him doubt Him... not the bullet lodged in Walt's body, not Walt being unconscious, not Dynasty being hauled off to jail. Nothing.

Praying as he walked over to the podium, Lamont truly believed that he felt the Lord guiding his steps. Taking a deep breath, he picked up the microphone and said, "Blessed be the name of the Lord Jesus, our healer and deliverer." People began lifting their hands and shouting their agreement. "I know that we have witnessed a tragic situation tonight, and I don't have any answers for you on why that woman decided to come here tonight and shoot Pastor Walt."

Lamont had suspicions, but since he didn't know the woman and had never seen her in Walt's presence, he would keep his thoughts to himself. "But the Lord has been dealing with me on some things that I believe I'm supposed to share with you all tonight. So, please take your seats and bear with me."

Half the chairs were empty. So, some might have left the moment the bullet was fired, fearing that the next bullet might have their name on it if they didn't get out of there. But for the people who were still in their seats, Lamont felt compelled to tell them what had been weighing so heavy on his heart. "Turn with me to the book of Joshua, chapter seven. Let's start at verse eleven."

Once they were there, Lamont read for their hearing the scriptures in the same way he had read them when God first directed him to them. "Christians have sinned..."

After reading, Lamont said, "What it all boils down to, is that we simply forgot that living holy is a mandate that God has for our lives. And now we sit around and wonder why so much tragedy and pain is happening in the world. Why God doesn't seem to be hearing our prayers? There's too much sin in Christiandom, that's why." Lamont answered. "Get the sin out and then God will dwell with us again."

He then turned his Bible to Psalm chapter thirty-two and

began reading: "*Blessed is he whose transgression is forgiven, whose sin is covered. Blessed is the man unto whom the Lord imputeth not iniquity, and in whose spirit there is no guile. I acknowledged my sin unto thee, and mine iniquity have I not hid. "I said, I will confess my transgressions unto the Lord; and thou forgavest the iniquity of my sin."*

After Lamont read the part about acknowledging his sin and about God forgiving him, he realized that he had been doing just that for years, as he would continually go to God about his guilt for how Sonya died. At that moment, Lamont truly accepted the fact that God had forgiven him and he wanted the same thing for other Christians.

He continued reading in the book of Psalm. He was now at verse six: "*For this shall every one that is godly pray unto thee in a time when thou mayest be found: surely in the floods of great waters they shall not come nigh unto him. Thou art my hiding place; thou shalt preserve me from trouble; thou shalt compass me about with songs of deliverance.*"

As Lamont closed his Bible, God had him look out at the lake and the vision of hundreds upon hundreds of people being baptized and renewed in their faith flashed before his eyes. He turned to the congregation with hope in his voice and said, "We have rented this space for the entire weekend, so I'm not going anywhere. What I'm going to ask you to do is join me in a consecration to the Lord."

When little interest was shown for Lamont's idea of a consecration, he lifted his head to heaven and then prayed for help. He then said to the people, "Aren't you tired of trying to cover up your sin? Are you tired of praying and receiving no answer? Don't you want to live holy?"

"Yes, yes and yes's were shouted throughout the pavilion as people began to stand up and move closer to the front.

"Then join me, saints. Let's consecrate ourselves from sin. Let's fast and pray and sing unto the Lord. Then on the last day of this revival," Lamont pointed out towards the lake where God had shown him a vision, "we are going to be baptizing any and all who have taken part in the consecration. And I guarantee you, saints, if you do this with me this weekend, God will rain down the power of the Holy Ghost like you've never seen it before."

The people began dancing and shouting as they were all prepared to fast, pray and wait on the Lord to renew their strength. Spirit filled saints were on the ground bowed down, thanking and praising God. They had known for a long time that the body of Christ needed a refreshing and had been praying for this very thing for many years. Reign, Lord Jesus, Reign, they all began to sing.

In the back of the room the cameramen kept rolling the tape. One of them had alerted The Word in Action Network as to what was going on and they were now on a live feed. Other networks were picking up their broadcast as well. During the eleven o'clock news, the word would be spread all across the town about the revival taking place at Edgewater Park.

TWENTY

"**I** should have shot him myself," Cynthia said as she sat with JT in the waiting room.

Walt was in surgery and Cynthia didn't appear to be devastated any longer. She was madder than a purse snatcher holding onto an empty purse. JT tried to calm her. "Don't say things like that, Cynthia. You don't mean it." JT tried to find a way to bring comfort to Cynthia, but that was a hard task, since he didn't know how to defend a man who had just been shot by his girlfriend in front of hundreds of people.

"Oh I mean it, all right. And don't act like you didn't see Victoria pull me off of Walt and start hugging on him as if he was her husband," she fumed, then balled her fist in anger as she said, "I feel like such a weakling for just sitting idly by and letting that woman shoot my husband for his cheating ways. I should have done it myself." She closed her eyes, shook her head. "I'm such a fool."

"I'm sorry for what has happened between you and Walt."

She shrugged as if nothing mattered anymore. "Oh, it's not like I don't deserve everything I got. After all, I'm the reason he became so power hungry in the first place, right?"

"This isn't your fault, Cynthia. Don't blame yourself for things that Walt did."

With a smirk on her face she told him, "I already know

that you blame me for everything. You're still ticked with me because I talked Walt into preaching rather than continuing to carry your Bible and water around."

JT lifted a hand, halting Cynthia's accusations. "You and Walt made the decision despite my counsel. I might not have agreed with it, but I stuck by the both of you throughout the years."

Cynthia lowered her head. She pulled some tissue out of the tissue box on the coffee table next to her and wiped her eyes. "I'm sorry for what I said. I'm just so angry right now that I can't think straight."

He patted her on the shoulder. "Don't worry about it. I'd be angry if someone shot my spouse also."

The doctor entered the waiting room and came up to Cynthia. "Mrs. Jenson?"

"Yes, that's me." Cynthia stood up. JT joined her as they waited for the doctor to speak.

"I'm Doctor Joseph Livingston. I just completed surgery on your husband and we were able to remove the bullet."

"Oh thank God," Cynthia said. "Is he all right?"

The doctor continued. "I understand that he was shot in the stomach, however, the bullet lodged into his back. And although we were able to get it out, I can't promise that he will be able to walk again."

"Oh my God." Cynthia slumped back into her chair with her hand over her mouth.

"Thanks for letting us know, Doctor," JT said and then sat back down next to Cynthia. "You can't give up, Cynthia. Trust God and believe that Walt will walk again."

"You don't understand," she said miserably. "I want to leave him." Crying like somebody stole something precious from her, she added, "Now I'm stuck. I'll have to take care of him for the rest of my life. You can't leave a crippled man, no matter how low-down he is… I'm being punished."

JT's cell rang at the right time. He knew how to comfort people who were grieving for their loved ones, but this whole grieving for self pity was new territory for him. Cassandra was calling and so he answered. "Hey honey, is everything okay?"

"JT, are you anywhere near a television?"

JT looked and saw a flat screen television hooked to the wall in the waiting room. "Yeah, there's a television in here."

"Turn on the news."

No one else was in the waiting room besides him and Cynthia, who was busy crying her eyes out for herself. So, JT got up and turned on the television. It was already on one of the local news channels. "I have it on; they're talking about the shooting."

"Keep watching," Cassandra told him. "The channel you're watching is probably getting ready to show the same thing I just saw on Channel 7."

JT did as he was told and after a minute the camera switch from showing Walt being placed in an ambulance and Dynasty in the police car, to Lamont standing behind the podium. He was saying, "Christians have sinned." The camera then switched back to the anchorman and he said, "You heard him right, folks. Someone is finally telling the truth on these holier-than-thou Christians. This preacher has called for consecration from sin for the entire weekend. And he even plans to baptize all who take part in the consecration on Sunday at Edgewater Park..."

"Did you see the faces of the people who were still at the revival?" Cassandra asked her husband.

"They look hungry... and not just for food, since Lamont just called a fast, but they look hungry for a move of God." JT got excited. "This is it, Sanni. This is what God has called Lamont to do."

"And it wouldn't have happened without you," Cassandra reminded him.

"I may have had the idea about the revival, but everything

Lamont said on that stage came from his time with God," JT corrected.

"No baby, I'm not talking about the message that Lamont delivered. I'm talking about the fact that Lamont wanted to pack up and go home after everything that happened tonight. But God used you to help Lamont see that he had to press on. And the whole city is getting the message. If you hadn't been there to give Lamont the shove he needed, there would be no move of God this weekend."

Humbly, JT said, "Thank you for saying that, Sanni. I'm glad that God saw fit to use me in whatever way he needed to."

"How are Walt and Cynthia doing?" Cassandra asked.

Running his hand through his wavy hair, JT said, "Walt's out of surgery. But I'm not real sure how Cynthia is doing. I was hoping that I could bring her home, so she can spend the night with us... and then maybe you can talk with her."

"Bring her on. I know I wouldn't want to be alone at a time like this."

"Thanks baby, we'll be there shortly."

When Margie was on the ground trying to stop Dynasty from shooting herself, she thought long and hard about fellowshipping with God by watching the televangelists. Coming to church was getting much too dangerous. But when Lamont stood up and proclaimed the word of God that it was time for the church to get right and that they were going into consecration, she knew that there was no way that she would miss this move of God.

She wasn't about to hide out in her bedroom watching this on television. Margie was determined to get everything she needed from God this weekend. But she also wanted so many more of God's children to partake in this time of consecration.

So, she went to her car and pulled out her iPad and began writing about this consecration period on her blog. After admonishing everyone to take part in the weekend fast and consecration to the Lord, she then told all of her blog followers...

> *I don't care where you live, you need to get to Cleveland, Ohio. Whether you have to get on a bus, train or plane to get here, if I were you, I would get here by Sunday for the baptism. I work for Pastor Lamont so I can testify that he is truly a man of God, so I believe him when he says that the power of the Holy Ghost will fall on us like never before after the baptism and renewal. See you all soon. And remember to stay prayed up!*

Margie knew that many of the people who read her blog were broken hearted because their faith and trust in God had been shaken after experiencing some manner of church hurt. She wanted them all to feel the power of God as he removed the guilt, shame and even the pain out of their lives.

After uploading the message to her blog, Margie closed down her iPad, put it back in her glove compartment and then went back into the church= to check on Lamont. She had already sent several deacons from Brother JT's and Lamont's churches to the grocery store to pick up a mountain load of bottled water. Margie wanted to make sure that she had Lamont covered.

He'd called a fast for the people, but it was warm outside, so she didn't want anyone to pass out. She understood that this was about consecration, but it never hurt to stay one step ahead of the scammers. After all, Margie's Bible told her that God had allowed the wheat to grow with the tares... in other words; everybody coming into the house of God wasn't saved.

Lamont was on his knees before the altar crying out to God. Margie noticed that the cameramen were still filming even though the room was quiet except for the people who were praying right now. She walked over to the cameramen and asked, "Why are you wasting all of your film? Why don't you just wait until Sunday and then film the baptism?"

"Are you joking?" one of the men asked.

"You must not know," the other added, "we are streaming live on the Internet and several Christian stations have cancelled their normal broadcasts and are carrying this event throughout the entire weekend."

"Oh my good God," Margie said. As she turned away from the cameramen and went to the front of the pavilion and sat down in an empty chair, she realized that this move of God was about to be even bigger than anything she could ever imagine.

TWENTY ONE

J T threw on a pair of black slacks and a button down white shirt. He kissed his wife and his children goodbye as they sat at the breakfast table with Cynthia.

"You're headed out already? " Cassandra asked.

"From what I was told, most of the people spent the night there, so I'm a bit late on arrival, don't you think?" JT said jokingly.

"Well at least sit down and have some breakfast before you go."

Shaking his head, JT reminded her, "Lamont called for a fast this weekend." He sniffed the air, taking in the aroma of pancakes and sausage. "It smells good in here, but I'm not about to break this fast until after the baptism on Sunday."

Cassandra put her hand to her mouth, and then quickly removed it. "Honey, I'm so sorry. I forgot all about the fast. But I haven't eaten yet, so I'm all in with you."

"Are you coming to the revival?" JT asked, hopeful that he and Cassandra could take part in this move of God together.

"Just let me feed the kids and get dressed. I'm going to drop the kids off with my Mom, then take Cynthia to get her car and sit with her at the hospital for a little while, but after that I will be at the revival with you for the rest of the weekend."

"Perfect," JT said to his wife, then he turned to Cynthia and said, "Please call my cell phone if you need me to do anything for Walt or you today. I know Cassandra will be sitting with you this morning. But if you need us to come back, just let me know."

Cynthia nodded and then stood up. "I appreciate that." She walked over to the stove and grabbed two sausage links. "I'm going to get dressed." She began chewing the sausage before she stepped out of the kitchen.

As JT entered the park, he knew without a shadow of a doubt that God was with them. The half could not be told of what God was doing in the lives of the people. Several Christian stations were streaming the event live. JT had even found a link online to watch the revival last night. But until he was actually standing there, he hadn't been able to fully comprehend just what this was. The power of the Holy Ghost fell on him, and JT began walking around the place prophesying, "Your change is coming... wait on the Lord and be of good cheer, for the God you seek is here, dwelling among you."

He then fell on his face, prostrate before God and began weeping and praying, praying and weeping.

The power of the Holy Ghost had not been limited to JT,because as more and more people arrived at the second day of consecration, one after another they would begin prophesying, telling one and all that the day of the Lord was near.

After hours of laying prostate before the Lord, a few of the choir members took the stage and began singing, "*He Wants It All.*" The singers were prophesying themselves as the song went on to tell the people that God walked over the earth and that He was longing for a child that would give Him their all.

When that song was finished, one of the choir members introduced a Michael W. Smith song to the congregation. Once they got the hang of the song, everyone began to understand the importance of the lyrics to *The Heart of Worship*. They all began to sing with a loud voice, telling God that they were coming back to the heart of worship. Because they now understood that worship was all about God.

A part of the song apologized for turning worship into something else, like a spectacle or a concert that really had nothing to do with God. But when they came to the lyrics that said, "I'm sorry Lord, for the things I've made it," tears began to flow, and instead of apologizing for not worshiping right, they began crying out to God, saying, "I'm so sorry, Lord. I want to live right... I'm sorry for taking Your grace and mercy for granted... I'm sorry, I'm sorry, I'm sorry," could be heard all across the park as the people earnestly cried out to God. At one point the music stopped, because the musicians were on their knees crying out their apologies to the Lord also. But the sweet song of those apologies didn't need a guitar or piano to make its way to heaven.

The Almighty was seated on His throne. His omnipotence glistened through the emerald rainbow arched above the magnificent throne. The twenty-four elders surrounded Him, who were also seated on thrones, and clothed in white radiant robes. They wore crowns of gold on their heads.

Seven lamps of fire were burning and a sea of crystal lay at the Master's feet. In the midst of the throne and around it, were four living creatures with eyes covering their entire bodies. The first living creature was like a lion, the second a calf, the third, a man, and the fourth, a flying eagle. Each of the creatures had six wings. They do not rest day or night, as their massive wings enable them to soar high above the thrones. Generating cool winds throughout heaven, they bellow continuous alms to their King crying, "Holy, holy, holy. Lord, God Almighty. Who was and is and is to come!"

The twenty-four elders fell down before Him and worshipped saying, "You are worthy, O Lord, to receive glory and honor and power; for You created all things, and by Your will they exist and were created." They threw their crowns before the throne in adoration. But even while all of this was going on, the Lovely One, the One who sits high but graciously looks low, heard the sweet sound of worship mixed with sorrow coming up from the earth.

Michael stood in the back of the throne room. He clasped his jewel embedded sword against the captain of the host and congratulated the angel on a job well done. The captain and his mighty warriors had just come back from a battle which had brought many souls to Christ in a region of the world where the Lord Jesus Christ was not accepted. "Your men have done well. They not only helped those preachers bring souls to Christ but they kept them alive also."

The captain put his sword back in its sheath and smiled. "The battle was well worth it."

The voice of thunder and lightning crackled from the throne. Michael excused himself. When he returned, he said, "The Lord has need of you again."

The captain unsheathed his sword once again and stood like a soldier ready for battle. "We will do the will of the Lord."

Michael patted the angel on the shoulder, comforted by the fact that he could count on this angel. Sounds are coming up from the earth that the Lord wants you and your host of angels to go down and check this out. If it truly is the sounds of repentance, then do everything in your power to help this young man with the task that God has put before him.

That evening JT received a call from an old friend, Pastor Isaac Walker from the House of God Christian Church. "Hey JT, I called to let you know that we are fasting and praying with you all. Nina and I have been watching the revival on television and we're just in awe of what God is doing down there."

"Thank you for praying for us, but I think we're really going to need some help with the baptism tomorrow. Lamont is calm now, but I don't think he has a clue what is about to break off in this place tomorrow."

"You think the crowd will be too much for you and Lamont to handle tomorrow?"

JT looked around the park and said, "Right now this place is filled to capacity. And from what I'm being told, we have hundreds more flying in for the conclusion of this revival. I'm actually surprised the fire marshal hasn't said anything." JT gave Isaac a correct assessment, but what he didn't tell his friend was about his fear that he wouldn't be able to help Lamont with the baptism tomorrow. God had already shown Lamont the blood that was on JT's hands because he had caused many in his congregation to sin, because of the sin filled life he had led at one time. So, JT needed to get Lamont some help.

"I'll tell you what I can do," Isaac said with a willing heart. "I'll see if one of my elders can preach tomorrow's sermon and then Nina and I will get on the road and come help out."

Excitedly, JT said, "Thanks brother. I really appreciate you. I had been in prayer about how we would handle the crowd tomorrow, so I know that your call was straight from God."

"I do enjoy being in tune with the Almighty," Isaac said. "See you soon."

Lamont grabbed the microphone and said, "I want everyone to grab a prayer partner. Now is the time to go to God concerning any loved ones who need a spiritual healing and ones who need a physical healing. Pray and call those names out before the Lord.

When he stepped down from the podium, Margie approached him and asked, "Can I partner with you?"

He held out his hands to her. "Who do you want to pray for?"

Margie told Lamont about the many people she came into contact with on her blog and suggested that they lift the broken hearted up in prayer. She also asked for prayer for her mother and other sideline victims of sin just like her.

Lamont nodded and as they went into prayer for those people, a chorus of prayers were going up, up, up to heaven all around the park, as others joined hands and agreed with each other in prayer that their loved ones would be saved, restored or healed, by the blood of Jesus. Amen.

When they were finished praying, JT grabbed the microphone, sat down at the edge of the stage and admonished the people to gather around, move as close as possible. But so many people had found their way to the park since yesterday that the pavilion could no longer hold the people. Thanks to the camera crew... it was now a crew, rather than just the two cameramen they started with on Friday night; they now had speakers that amplified their voices to every corner of the park. Those who were not at the park, were able to watch everything unfold from the comfort of their homes on television or online.

"I'd like to tell you the story of a man who thought he could hide his iniquities from God, but instead ended up causing so much harm to the body of Christ that it has taken him years to repair." JT was talking about himself. He told the story of how he'd lost faith in God after the death of his first child, but instead of stepping down from the pulpit and allowing God to heal his heart, he began whore mongering.

Cassandra came and sat down next to her husband. And as tears of shame dampened his cheeks, she wiped them away, signaling to everyone that she and her husband were in this together. "So you see my brothers and sister," JT continued. "I don't judge Pastor Walt Jenson for what happened to him, because I can't. What I am asking is that we all come together and pray for Walt's recovery, in mind body and spirit. And pray for his wife, Cynthia."

The people came together in prayer again. As the night wore on, more people stood up, grabbed the microphone and began testifying about sin that they had been involved in, but by the grace of God they truly felt as if they had been changed by attending this revival.

Like a good son, Tony had brought his mother back to the revival the second night. They hadn't made it there in time to get one of the seats in the pavilion, but as they sat on lawn chairs in the park, fellowshipping with others, he heard JT's confessions and truly believed that the pastor was now a changed man. At that moment, in front of all the people around them, Tony began to weep as he wondered if the Lord could possibly change his life also.

Tony wasn't the only one wondering about the Lord's power to change to lives. Lying in his hospital bed, Walt had listened to everything JT said. He was thankful that JT had said kind things about him and then asked everyone to pray for him. Walt could feel those prayers and it humbled him.

Walt turned his face to the wall and with tears glistening in his eyes and a heavy heart, he began his journey back to God.

TWENTY TWO

In the early morning hours of the third day, the angels of the Lord descended and began walking on what they now knew to be holy ground. The sounds the Lord heard were true. People were earnestly praying and calling out to Him. For a long while now, the angels of the Lord wondered if the Church of Christ could stand once it had been infiltrated with so much ungodly sin. But they were witnessing a rebirth. Captain Aaron was thankful that he would be able to give a good report once they returned back to heaven.

The angels had full view of everything that was going on in the park, but they themselves were unseen to human eyes. They walked into the pavilion. Lamont and JT were stretched out before the altar praying. Standing between the two men, Aaron felt the presence of God. He touched both men, strengthening them for the task that was before them. "You're almost there, don't give in now."

Three prominent pastors, known all over the world for the great works they had done were having a feast of a breakfast at the Ritz Carlton in Cleveland, Ohio. Big slabs of ham, turkey bacon, eggs, french toast and home fries dressed their plates... meals fit for kings. And why not, they were at one of the finest luxury hotels in America, and they could well afford to be there.

One preacher was pastor at a church in Texas, New York and Atlanta. He broadcasted live from one of the churches two times a week. The other was a faith healer who had drawn people to him by the thousands with his healing ministry. God had blessed his hands to heal the sick and cause the lame to walk... that is, until he began to believe that he, and not God was the healer. The last preacher came from a long line of pastors and from a child, he knew that he would serve the Lord all of his days. He founded his first church with only twenty members, most of which had been his wife and children. But as God began to bless, the attendance grew to twenty thousand members every Sunday. He now had a television and radio ministry as well as the numerous conferences he held each year.

Once they had eaten and were full, the multiple church pastor said, "We really should have fasted this morning."

The mega church pastor silenced that notion. "We have all been in the ministry for over twenty years and have each fasted more than that little youngster down at that park will ever have an occasion to do. So, I see no reason to starve ourselves now... not when God himself has given us the provisions to eat and live as well as we so choose."

The healer nodded his agreement as he finished drinking his orange juice. "Bless the Lord for the provisions." He wiped his mouth with his napkin and then said, "Now, how about we get on down to that park and be of help to this young man with all the work that will need to be done today."

"Amen to that," Mega pastor said, then added. "And just in case you haven't thought of it, I emailed my assistant when we arrived in town last night and told her to alert the media that I would be helping with the baptism today."

"Good idea," Multi-church pastor said, as he pulled out his iPhone and sent a quick email to his own assistant.

The healer did the same, then stood up. "Well, let's get going."

The three wonderful men of God walked out of the restaurant and up to the concierge desk to find out if their limousine was ready for them. The concierge informed them that the car wasn't ready, because no one had informed him of the time they would be leaving for Edgewater Park.

Multi-church pastor exploded, "Are you kidding me? Is this a joke?"

"No sir," the small man said from behind the desk. "I would never kid around with such important men as you and your friends. But if you can give me a few minutes, I'm sure I can have a car ready for you."

The healer asked, "Will it be the limo? Because I'm not interested in riding in anything less."

"Yes, sir, I'll get it ready for you momentarily," the man said and then hurried to get his job done for his important clients.

JT and Isaac clasped hands as they smiled at each other. "It's been too long," JT said.

"Yes, it's been way too long," Cassandra agreed as she and Nina hugged and then began walking with their husbands.

It was eight in the morning, so JT and Lamont were getting ready to pray and then begin taking people down to the lake. "You and Nina arrived right on time, but I should have known that you would."

"To tell you the truth, I could barely sleep last night. I couldn't wait to take part in this move of God and I was thrilled that you asked me to come and help."

"And we're thrilled to have you," JT told him as they entered the pavilion.

Lamont was waiting for them at the front of the church. He had this awestruck look on his face. When JT and Isaac approached he said, "Did you all notice how many people are here?"

"The place is so packed, you'd think President Obama was speaking this morning," Isaac said as he shook Lamont's hand. "How are you doing?"

"I was fine until my assistant came over and told me that we have sick people lined up by the lake believing that God is going to trouble the waters so that all manner of sickness and disease will be healed," Lamont said.

If that's what the people came expecting, then that is what you and JT should be praying for... remember, our God is a wonder worker," Isaac encouraged.

"I haven't seen many wondrous things since founding my ministry. But I believe that God is about to change all that today." He nodded. "Let's pray."

O n orders from on high, the captain of the host stood on the banks of the lake and put his sword in the water with one hand and then he lifted the other hand toward heaven. As he did that, the calm waters began to ripple.

A crippled man in a wheelchair was seated next to the lake. As the water rippled he turned to his son and said, "Didn't I tell you that God was going to get me out of this chair today?"

"Yeah Dad, you did. I think the pastors will be down in a minute to start the baptism."

"No son, I don't think I should wait. Throw me in the water right now."

Shaking his head, the boy said, "I can't do that, Dad. If you start drowning, I'm not strong enough to pull you out."

The crippled man began scooting his chair toward the water. "You won't have to pull me out. Now come on and trust me on this one." But as he continued to scoot closer to the lake and the water touched his feet, the man felt a tingle up his spine and then lifted himself from his chair and went into the water head first.

"Oh my God," Walt said as he watched the miracle unfold right before his eyes.

"What's wrong?" Cynthia asked waiting, she sat up in the cushiony chair she had slept in the night before. "Are you in pain?"

Walt pointed at the television. He was watching the revival. Lamont and Isaac Walker had just entered the lake and were now baptizing the thousands of people at the lake, one by one. But what had caught Walt's attention was the crippled man who had jumped in the lake, swam around and then when he got out, closed up his wheelchair and screamed, "I won't be needing this anymore... blessed be the name of the Lord!"

"Go get the doctor. I need to get down to that lake," Walt said with excitement in his voice. He had been watching the revival on television from the moment he woke from his surgery. He'd cried, prayed and repented along with everyone else and now Walt felt as if he was a new man and desperately wanted to be baptized as an outward showing of what had taken place inside of his heart and soul this weekend.

"Walt, the doctor is not going to release you. They want to move you to rehab so you can work on regaining the feeling in your legs," Cynthia said while rolling her eyes at the absurdity of his comment.

Walt ignored her skepticism and hit the nurse button.

When the nurse entered the room, he told her, "I need to see my doctor because I want to be released this morning."

"Dr. Livingston has requested rehab for you," the nurse said with a patient smile on her face.

Walt waved that notion away. "I don't need rehab. I need to get back to the revival and get into that water." He was pointing at the television as Lamont and Isaac were wading in the water and dunking one person after the next.

The nurse watched as women, men and children were pulled out of the water, jumping, shouting and speaking in tongues. "That's right, you were at that revival on Friday weren't you?" the nurse asked.

Walt sat up in bed with a mischievous grin on his face. "Wasn't much of a revival until I got shot. I hear they really got the party started while I was in surgery. But I can't let them end this revival without me."

The nurse opened her mouth to say something, then stopped. "I'll call your doctor and see if he will okay your release."

Walt threw the covers off and said, "Just know that if he doesn't okay it, I'm getting ready to be AWOL."

Thousands of people had come to the park on the last day of the consecration and baptism. They had either walked, driven or taken planes from other cities in Ohio or another state all together. Wherever they came from, they were all lined up at the lake now. Many of them had given their lives to the Lord and been baptized years ago. However, they hadn't lived their lives according to the will of God. This weekend, during the revival, they had made a decision to turn back to God and live right. So, now they wanted to be re-baptized as an outward showing of what had taken place in their hearts.

They had spent the weekend praying, fasting and repenting. Those that desired salvation were sent to altar workers so they could pray the sinner's prayer and receive Christ into their lives and then they were brought back to the line to await the baptism.

One by one, Lamont and Isaac said, "I baptize you in the name of the Father, the Son and the Holy Ghost, all in Jesus name." And then they dunked the person who stood before them. They had been at it for a few hours, but the line didn't seem to be getting any shorter. If anything, it seemed to be getting longer. Lamont lifted his head toward heaven and prayed for strength.

Then Stephanie and Marcus, two of his church members

that had been through the storm stepped in front of him, hand in hand and asked him to baptize them. With renewed strength, Lamont gladly baptized them and praised God for bringing them back home, where they belonged.

The three pastors who wanted to come to the revival to help out were at that moment sitting on the side of the road. The limo they were riding in somehow had two flat tires. The limo driver used the spare in the trunk of the car to change one tire, but once he put the flat in his trunk and exhaled, he noticed that the back tire on the opposite side of the car was also flat. "What the devil?" he was truly perplexed as to what was going on.

But if he had been able to see in the spirit, he would have known that the devil had nothing to do with it. An angel of the Lord had flattened both tires, because God was not willing to share His glory this day.

He opened the back door of his limo, he hesitated for a moment and then said, "I have another flat."

"What? Don't you service these vehicles on a regular schedule?" The pastor was outraged.

"I do apologize for this, pastors. I know that you're trying to get to that revival, so I can call a cab for you while I get this problem sorted out."

"Boy, do you know who I am?" Without waiting for an answer, the healer said, "I am a servant of the Most High, and I don't ride in cabs."

The limo driver wiped his brows with his handkerchief. "Okay, well, I can get you there; it's just going to be a while."

"That's fine, young man, just turn the air conditioning back on," The multi-church pastor said. He had paid too many dues to be doing all this sweating. These days he hired people to do the sweating for him.

JT was helping people into the lake, careful to stay away from the actual baptism. He did not want the blood on his hands to rub off on anyone as they were in the water trying to get their deliverance, healing or just a rejuvenation. But as he watched Lamont and Isaac struggle to handle the massive crowd that did not seem to be diminishing, he got down on his knees at the edge of the water, lifted his hands to God and prayed, "Lord, these hands desire to work for You. I understand about the blood that is on my hands because of the sin that I committed, just as King David had blood on his hands because of the many wars he waged. But I don't live in the days of King David... I live in the days of grace and mercy, because of your son, Jesus. So, I ask that you take the blood from my hands so that I can be of use in your kingdom."

As JT prayed, an angel stood behind him with fire in his hands. He leaned down and touched the hands that JT lifted to the Lord.

As JT's hands connected with the angel's, he felt the heat go through his hands and then warm his whole body. And then a swift wind blew a tidal wave of water over his body and sent him tumbling to the bottom of the lake. JT held his breath as he swam back up to shore. As his head lifted out of the water, JT realized that he had just been fire baptized. And the Lord had cleansed him from the inside out.

He wanted to take a little time to shout and jump and scream over what the Lord had just done for him, but there was no time for that now. The line was growing longer, and Lamont and Isaac needed help. JT waded into the water and stood to the left of Lamont and bade the people to come his way. Now three of God's men stood baptizing and calling what was once unholy, holy again.

TWENTY THREE

"What is taking that doctor so long?" Walt questioned after waiting two hours to be released from the hospital.

"I'm sure the man has other patients, Walt. You're not the president of the United States. He doesn't have to drop everything he's doing to come and answer your crazy questions," Cynthia said while flipping through a magazine and trying her best to look any and everywhere but at her husband.

Walt slowed his roll and looked at his wife for a moment. He had loved Cynthia from the moment he'd seen her. Had been willing to do anything to please her. And then somehow, as the years wore on, he'd only been interested in pleasing himself. He had a lot of making up to do for the pain he'd caused her. Walt just prayed that he hadn't come to his senses too late. Adjusting himself in the bed, he told her, "I get that you are ticked with me."

She put the magazine in her lap and gave him an 'oh really' stare. Then she said, "You must be a genius if you get the reason I'm ticked off. Because I doubt if any other woman in this world would be angry if her husband's woman shot him and then his other woman pulled her away from her husband while she's trying to comfort him."

Ouch. He was trying to find something to say to that when she continued.

"And now, lucky me, I get to take care of you for the rest of my life."

Walt lifted a hand. "No, you shouldn't be stuck taking care of me. The only thing I'm asking from you is that you get me to this revival... I have a feeling that God has a blessing for me out there. Can you do that for me?"

"What is taking so long, it seems as if we're just traveling in circles?" The healer rolled down the window that separated them from the driver and asked.

"Honestly sir, I do not know. My GPS says that the park is about one block over, but every time I drive over there, I can't figure out where to let you off, because I can't see the park."

Mega church pastor was on the phone with his assistant. She was saying, "I've received calls from numerous radio and television stations. They have been trying to find you at the revival so they can get a quick interview."

"I know that," he snapped. "I'm trying to get to the park, but this idiot driver doesn't know how to follow a GPS. Instead of driving us around, he needs to be riding on a little short bus."

The other two pastors laughed at the insult. Then one of them told the driver, "Just take us back to the spot your GPS has directed you to and let us out." He then rolled up the window and rolled his eyes to high heaven.

The driver drove back to the place he'd circled around for the last hour and opened the door for the men. "Have a nice day," he said with a smile. Even though his shoulders were slumped.

As the three preachers got out of the limo, they were able to see clearly that the park was in front of them. The preachers opened their mouths to give the driver one last piece of their minds, but then one of the preachers saw reporters headed their way and zipped it.

The driver got back in his car and sped off.

The preachers turned back toward the park after the driver left. At that moment they saw what their driver had been seeing... absolutely nothing. The angel that stood in front of them blocked their view so that they couldn't see the miraculous things that were taking place on that day.

By the time Cynthia arrived at the park with Walt, the line had finally gone down. Walt prayed that he hadn't arrived too late for God to do a miracle in him. Cynthia took the wheelchair they left the hospital with out of the trunk of her car and helped Walt into it. She pushed him down to the lake where a multitude of people stood around, dripping wet and smiling from the joy of it all. JT, Lamont and Isaac were in the water, baptizing all who came forward. As she pushed Walt closer and closer to the lake, she witnessed Margie run over to Lamont and then she saw him dunk her down deep into the water, as she came up, she was laughing and crying at the same time.

Cynthia turned toward Isaac and in front of him stood Tony Denario. Tony lifted his hands, appeared to be reciting words after Isaac and then he was taken low into the water. She frowned as Tony came up speaking in tongues, for she knew what a horrid life he had led.

"Push me up to the edge of the water," Walt said.

"All right, but if you fall in, don't blame me."

As Walt reached the edge of the water, JT looked up and saw his old armor bearer and friend. He had prayed that Walt would find his way out there today, but since JT didn't know what condition the man's heart was in, he'd left all of that up to God. But as he looked directly into Walt's eyes, JT knew without a shadow of a doubt that God had worked on Walt's heart that weekend. He rushed over to him and bent down in front of Walt. "I'm surprised that the doctor let you go so soon."

"I can be mighty persuasive when I need to be. I'm doped up on pain killers right now, but I wasn't going to let that stop me from participating in this miraculous event." Walt put his hand on JT's shoulder and asked, "Would you baptize me, Pastor?"

JT smiled. "Has God touched your heart this weekend?"

"In ways you couldn't even imagine. I have been so wrong and God helped me to see that this weekend." Tears streamed down Walt's eyes. "I truly want to live for Him." Walt pointed toward heaven.

JT had Lamont help him lift Walt out of the wheelchair. They carried him into the water. JT said, "I baptize you in the name of the Father, the Son, and the Holy Ghost... all in Jesus' matchless and magnificent name." At that point he dunked Walt until he could be dunked no further, as he brought him up, Walt began to squirm in his arms.

"Let me go," Walt told JT.

JT did as he was commanded and Walt swam in the water like a fish born to it. As he circled back around, he stood up next to JT. He was still crying as he said, "I told that nurse I wasn't going to need physical therapy."

JT hugged him. "Boy, you are truly a wonder. Good to have you back."

"And I'm glad to be back."

Cassandra and Nina got in the water. The crowd was winding down, and they were not going to miss their blessing. Cassandra asked JT to baptize her and Nina asked Isaac.

Walt looked around for Cynthia. When he spotted her, he could tell that she had become emotional over his healing because she was crying. But what he didn't understand was the fact that Cynthia hadn't ran into the water as Cassandra and Nina had. She was headed in the opposite direction, back to the car.

Walt got out of the water and followed after his wife. "Cynthia, Cynthia," he called.

She didn't stop, just kept crying and walking away from him.

Walt caught up with her in the parking lot. "What's wrong, baby? Why don't you come back and let JT baptize you?"

She shook her head and turned away from him.

Walt held onto her arm. "Cynthia, please don't leave. I know I messed up,but I believe we can work this out... I'm planning on quitting the ministry."

She turned to him in amazement. "But I can see the glow of God all over you. How can you leave God now?"

Walt shook his head. "I'm not leaving God. I plan to serve Him for the rest of my life, in whatever capacity God chooses, but I'm not called to be a pastor... I think you know that. I sure figured it out."

She turned away from him again and unlocked her car door.

"Things will be better for us now, Cynthia, I promise you that. Just give me a chance."

She opened the car door, but just before getting in, she said, "You just don't get it do you?"

"Get what? Whatever is wrong, God can fix it, just give us a chance," he pleaded.

She closed her eyes for a moment and shook her head. When she focused on Walt again she admitted, "I paid a man to shoot you in the head this weekend. If your girlfriend hadn't shot you in the stomach, you would be dead right now." With that, she got in her car and drove out of his life.

The sun was going down as Lamont baptized Margie's mom and then the last few people in line. The captain of the host lifted his sword from the water and he and the other angels that had diligently guarded the park so that the work of the Lord could be done, ascended back up into heaven just as quickly as they had descended.

Lamont looked out at the crowd of people who were still hanging around and said with a loud voice, "The Lord showed Himself mighty here today, now hear the command of the Lord... don't ever forget to live holy again. Let your light shine before men, so that they will see and want to know more about the hope that lives in you."

EPILOGUE

JT and Cassandra went out to dinner with Isaac and Nina. They had worked hard and long so they enjoyed their time of fellowship together as they broke the fast. Lamont had begged off, saying that he was so tired, he just wanted to go home and sleep for a month.

After dinner, that was exactly what JT wanted to do, also. Cassandra drove him home, while he rested his eyes. As she pulled into their driveway, she tapped him on the shoulder. "We have company."

"Say it ain't so," JT said as he opened his eyes and caught sight of Diane sitting on their porch. He said again, "Say it ain't so."

"Make this quick, JT. This has been a long, eventful weekend and I am tired, too."

JT put his hand on his wife's arm, leaned over and kissed her on the cheek and then said, "Let's go see what she has to say."

They got out of the car, and as they approached Diane, Cassandra said, "The kids aren't here. We left them with my mom this weekend."

Diane stepped off the porch, and walked towards them. "I figured the kids wouldn't be here." Then to explain her comment she said, "I watched the rest of the revival on television."

"I wish you had come back, the baptisms we did today were something out of this world. God really blessed today," JT said.

Diane nodded. "I know He did. Look, I just came by to apologize for the way I've been acting. And to tell you and Cassandra that things will be different from now on."

Both JT and Cassandra were speechless for a moment.

Diane continued. "Well, anyway, that's all I wanted to say." She walked down the driveway, got in her car and drove off.

JT put his arm around Cassandra and pulled her closer to him as he said, "The Lord really did bless today."

Cassandra kissed the tip of his nose. "Sure did, Pastor Thomas, He sure did."

Lamont had stayed at the park a little longer than expected. He sat at the bank of the lake, taking in the calmness of the water. It hadn't been so calm an hour ago. The wind and the waves had been ever flowing as they baptized one believer after the next. At that moment, Lamont smiled, because God had answered his prayers... He had troubled the water and brought physical and spiritual healing to His people.

"Young man."

Lamont heard someone calling out to him. He looked up and saw three prominent preachers that he looked up to and had even reworded a few of their sermons. He stood and wiped off his pants. "Pastors," he said, with excitement in his voice at seeing them.

"We have been walking around for hours trying to find the place where the baptisms are being done. We came to help with the work of the Lord. Can you help us find the location?" Pastor Larry asked.

"I'm so sorry that you missed it, but God has already finished His work today. Everyone has been baptized and they have gone home with victory."

At hearing this the three men turned with slumped shoulders and went away without thanking Lamont for the good news.

A bit bewildered by the actions of the three preachers, Lamont made the climb back up the hill and through the park toward his car with a grumble in his stomach. As his car came into view, so did Margie. She was sitting on the hood of his car holding a picnic basket. Lamont smiled, that woman was always anticipating his needs. As he moved towards her, Lamont felt as if he was moving towards his destiny.

Margie got off the hood of his car and held out the basket to him. "It's time for you to eat."

With a mischievous grin, he said, "I can think of something that I need more than food right now."

"What's that?"

Lamont stepped to her, took the picnic basket out of her hands and set it on the hood of his car. He looked into her eyes as he said, "I need you in my life. I want to marry you, Margie, can you handle that?"

"B-but."

He bent down and kissed her softly on the lips. "No need to stutter, hon. God has shown me that you are the one for me."

Tears streamed down Margie's face as she hugged Lamont. "I thought something was wrong with me for feeling the way I've been feeling about you."

As Margie released Lamont from the hug, he said, "I only have one request, Margie."

"Tell me what you need."

Lamont put his arm around her as he walked her to the passenger side of his car. As he opened the door for her he said, "No more fights at church, okay?"

Margie blushed. "I just retired my boxing gloves."

The End

FORGIVEN

Book II in the *Forsaken Series*

PROLOGUE

Crouched down between a rusty old Lincoln with a play-boy symbol on the driver's side door and a red Pontiac with a busted rearview window, while a maniac wielded a tire iron that had already clipped her in the leg once, Diane Benson decided it was time to call her husband and beg for his forgiveness.

She had left Cleveland, Ohio about eight months ago after leaving her three oldest children with her husband, Joe Benson. She then drove to Pastor JT Thomas' house and left her three month old daughter with him and his wife. The way Diane saw it, every child needed to be with his or her own daddy and she didn't care how JT and Cassandra's life was disrupted. JT got what he deserved anyway. What kind of man pastors a church while sleeping with the deacon's wife? But JT hadn't only been sleeping with her. Diane could have understood if he had slipped into sin because he just couldn't resist her voluptuous curves and Angelina Jollie pouty lips. But that hadn't been the case.

JT would sleep with anything in a knee high skirt willing to kick her pumps off and get busy. Too bad she got pregnant before she figured that one out. She had been prepared to leave her husband for JT so they could start a new life with their baby. But JT suddenly developed a conscious and realized that a husband's place was at home with his wife. He expected her to just continue living a lie with Benson. JT never imagined that she would tell Benson the truth. But she had, and Benson beat the snot out of him.

Soon after JT got his beat down, Diane had become fed up with the whole matter. So after dropping Lily off with her daddy, she left town with Brian Johnson. Brian had been the mechanic at the auto dealership her husband owned. But Brian was fixing more than automobiles and Joe hadn't had a clue about it. Brian had been her side kick. When JT wasn't acting right, she spent her free time with Brian. She may have imagined herself as first lady of Faith Outreach while fooling around with JT, but Brian was the one who made her weak at the knees. She couldn't lie if she wanted to, that man held some type of demonic power over her and she lived to do his bidding. Actually, Lily could have been Brian's baby just as well as JT's. But Brian said that since she had been sleeping with JT more than him around the time that she'd gotten pregnant, Lily more than likely belonged to JT. Funny thing was, when the DNA test came back and it proved that Brian had been right; JT was Lily's father, Brian got so mad that he up and left her in Jacksonville, Florida with only twenty dollars to her name.

That's when she met Darryl Mills. Darryl was a house flipper. Since the economy turned and not many people were buying homes, he'd given Diane the key to a fabulous four bedroom home in the suburbs. Diane loved the house and was trying to figure out how she could convince Darryl to give it to her instead of putting it back on the market. Diane almost had Darryl convinced, until his nosy wife figured out that she was living in the house rent free. That's why Diane was crouched between two cars right now. The maniac with the tire iron was Darryl's wife.

"You might as well come out from between these cars. 'Cause I really don't care if I bang these cars up, just as long as you get banged up in the process."

Crawling on the ground, trying to move further into the jam packed parking lot and away from the tire iron, Diane said, "I don't even know you, lady. Why are you doing this?"

"You know me well enough to sleep with my husband," the woman said as she angled her obese body between the two closely parked cars and swung at Diane.

Thankful that the woman missed her that time, Diane stood up and ran as quickly as she could through the maze of cars.

Darryl's wife was simply too big to move any further in between the Lincoln and the Pontiac, so she couldn't catch Diane, but she screamed as loud as she could, "I'm throwing all your stuff out of my house and onto the street. If you come back here to get any of it, I'm going to shoot you."

Once Diane was a safe distance away from certain death, she used the cell phone that Darryl bought her to call Benson. When he answered she said, "Hey, Joe, I was just calling to check on the kids. How are they doing?"

"They miss you, Diane, that's how they're doing," Joe told her.

"I know. I know," she said, like a woman who'd learned her lesson. "I should have never left them. I miss all my babies."

"You received court papers about a custody hearing for Lily last week."

"What?" she said as if she couldn't believe this was happening to her. "What am I supposed to do, Joe? I don't even have a way to get back to Cleveland right now."

"The hearing is next month. I'll get you an airline ticket. Just tell me where you are."

That's what she wanted to hear, but she tried to tamper down her excitement as she said, "I don't know, Benson. The only reason I didn't turn around and come right back home eight months ago was because I was scared about how you would treat me."

Benson was almost seven feet tall, bulky and strong, but

with his wife, he might as well have been a midget. "Have I ever given you a reason to fear me? It's not just the kids missing you, Diane. I miss you. Just come home."

"What about Lily? I can't just forget that I have another child."

"I wasn't sure that you wanted Lily since you left her with JT."

"She's my child," Diane said angrily. JT wasn't just going to run over her with some custody hearing, telling some judge that his wife would be a better mother than she was.

Benson cleared his throat. "Just come home, Diane. We can work on getting Lily back from JT once we're back together."

"Okay, Benson. I'm in Jacksonville, Florida. Go online and order the ticket and I'll pick it up at the airport." Diane smiled as she hung up the phone. Benson had always been at her beck and call. She would go home, but she would also make JT pay for the agony she felt had been inflicted on her because of his refusal to leave his wife and marry her. And she would start by taking Lily away from him.

ONE

"What are you doing?" Mattie Davis asked when she walked into her daughter's bedroom and saw her throwing her clothes into a suitcase.

Cassandra Thomas turned to face her mother. With a smile on her face she said, "I'm going home."

Looking heavenward, Mattie proclaimed, "Lord, Jesus, my child has lost her mind again." Mattie sat down on the edge of Cassandra's bed. Her head was bowed low as she shook it from side to side. "Why do you want to ruin your life? I don't understand this at all."

"Stop being so dramatic, Mother. I've been away from JT for six months. It's time I went home."

JT Thomas had once been the pastor of Faith Outreach Church, but once his sins had been exposed, he'd been suspended and then he resigned from his position. JT was now restored back to God and an upstanding citizen who went to work at a community center everyday and held a monthly Bible study in his home for men struggling with infidelity and he'd also just started his own church. And yes, Cassandra was willing to admit it; she had fallen in love with her husband all over again. So why shouldn't she and her two sons, Jerome and Aaron, go back home where they belonged?

"I suppose this means you're willing to be a mother to that child he had while still married to you," Mattie stated.

"Yes, Mother, I will be just as much Lily's mother as I am Jerome and Aaron's. I've thought long and hard about this, and the way I see it, if another woman was willing to be a mother to me after you and Bishop Turner fooled around and had me, then how can I deny a child my love, just because I didn't give birth her?"

Mattie's shoulders' slumped. "You enjoy throwing that in my face, don't you? Okay, I made a mistake. Your father was a married man. But does that mean you have to pay for my sins for the rest of your life?"

Cassandra sat down next to her mother and put her arm around her shoulder. Her mother was a petite woman of little more than five feet, but she had a loud, boisterous voice that made her seem seven feet tall at times. "I'm not trying to throw anything in your face, but I'm in a predicament and I need your help to get out of it."

"What predicament? What are you talking about?"

"Well, it seems to me that you and Bishop Turner did to Susan what JT and Diane Benson did to me. Susan forgave you and Bishop and found a way to continue loving her husband. All I'm asking for is the chance to do the same thing with my husband."

"But how can you forgive what that man has done to you?" Mattie asked, refusing to see that she had done the same thing to another man's wife.

"The same way that I forgave you for all the years you lied to me about who my father was. The way I see it, Mother, forgiveness is a choice." Cassandra stood up, zipped her suitcase and pulled it off the bed. "Thank you for putting up with me and the boys for all these months, but I'm going home, Mother."

Cassandra put her key in the lock and opened the door. She stood in the entryway and looked around the modest home. It was certainly not the five bedroom, seven thousand square foot home she shared with JT before moving in with her mother. JT had sold their home after she moved in with her mother. He moved back into the first home they purchased together. It was only thirteen hundred square feet with three bedrooms and a basement, but Cassandra had loved everything about this home. Jerome and Aaron ran into the house and started screaming for JT.

When JT walked from the kitchen into the living room, the boys ran to him. He bent down and Jerome and Aaron jumped on him. "Daddy, Daddy, guess what?" Jerome said.

Laughing, JT said, "I can't guess, so please hurry up and tell me."

"We're home for good!" Jerome shouted.

"You are?" JT asked playfully.

"Yes, Mom said so." Jerome turned to Cassandra and asked, "Isn't that right, Mom? No more sleeping at granny's house during the week and here on the weekends. We get to be here with Daddy all the time now, don't we?"

The excitement in her son's voice brought tears to Cassandra's eyes. How she wished that she had never moved him away from his father, but at the time, she had no idea that she would ever come home again. So she and JT had agreed on shared custody. Just as Jerome had said, she had the boys during the week and JT had them on the weekend. "Yes, honey, we are home for good."

JT smiled as he stood and walked over to Cassandra. "I made dinner."

"You did not," Cassandra said as she put down her suitcase and walked into the kitchen. Not once, in the nine years she and JT had been married, had he ever volunteered to fix dinner. He expected his meals to be on the table the minute he was ready to eat, but he didn't bother to help with anything remotely related to kitchen duties.

As Cassandra lifted the lid on the skillet, JT said, "It's just Hamburger Helper."

"No," Cassandra said as she grinned from ear to ear, "what we have here is a miracle."

"Do you think the boys are ready to eat?" JT asked Cassandra.

"They haven't had anything since lunch, so I'm sure they're ready. What about Lily, is she sleeping?"

"Yeah. I put her down for a nap a while ago though, so I better go check on her."

Cassandra put her hand on JT's arm as she said, "No, let me go check on her."

"Okay, if you're going to get Lily, I'll help the boys wash their hands."

"Mr. Helpful, huh? Be careful, JT, I just might get used to this," Cassandra told him as she headed upstairs.

Lily was sitting up in her baby bed. Her big brown eyes were filling with tears as she opened her mouth to proclaim that she was awake and didn't appreciate being left alone. Cassandra took her out of the baby bed and held her close as she rocked the screaming child.

"There, there, Lily, it's not that bad." Cassandra sat down in the chair next to Lily's bed and continued to hold the child until her sobs subsided. She saw JT's features in Lily, just as she saw them in Jerome and Aaron. Funny thing was, looking at Lily and knowing that JT was her father didn't bother Cassandra anymore. Now she knew for sure that she was ready to be a mother to Lily. She began to sing to her, "*There's a Lily in the valley and you're bright as the morning star.*"

JT hollered up the stairs, "The boys are starving, are you two coming down so we can eat?"

"Sounds like your daddy is starving and trying to blame it on the boys." Cassandra bounced Lily on her lap and then said, "Come on, honey, let's go eat,"

JT was standing at the bottom of the stairs waiting on them. "What were you two doing up there?"

Cassandra rubbed JT's stomach as she put her feet on the bottom step. "Sorry, I forgot how hungry you get."

"I'm a growing man. I need to eat on the regular."

The boys were seated at the octagon shaped table that was only big enough for four chairs. Cassandra placed Lily in her high chair and then told JT, "We need to pick up Aaron's high chair from my mother's house in the morning. He really isn't big enough to sit at the table." Only six months had passed since she last lived with JT, so the children hadn't grown all that much. Jerome was now four years old, Aaron was eighteen months and Lily was ten months.

"Yeah, he does look a little awkward in that chair," JT said as he watched his son's legs dangle in the air. They were about two feet away from the ground, so there was no way that Aaron would be able to get out of that chair without help. JT put a plate of Hamburger Helper in front of each child.

"You help Aaron and I'll feed Lily," Cassandra told JT.

Dinner was a big hit. The boys absolutely loved it. Lily's noodles and hamburger pieces had to be chopped up, but she loved the meal as well. After dinner, the family watched TV in the family room until bath time. Cassandra was bathing Aaron and Lily when JT walked into the bathroom with her suitcase.

"This was still by the front door. Does it have the boys' stuff in it or yours?"

Cassandra pulled Lily out of the tub and started drying her off. "Some of my clothes are in that suitcase. I knew the boys had clothes here, so I figured we could go pack up their stuff together."

"That's fine. I'll just put your suitcase in our bedroom."

Alarm registered on Cassandra's face. She lifted her hand to halt JT. "Let me finish up with the kids before we make any decisions."

With a raised eyebrow, JT said, "What decisions?"

She finished drying Lily, handed her to JT and then took Aaron out of the tub and dried him off. "Let's put them to bed and then we can talk."

They put the kid's pajamas on and then laid them in their beds. Jerome had already bathed and was sound asleep. JT grabbed Cassandra's hand and pulled her out of Jerome and Aaron's room. "Let's talk."

They walked into their bedroom. Cassandra saw her suitcase in the corner and froze. JT gently pulled her the rest of the way into the room. "What's wrong?" JT asked.

"Nothings wrong, I just thought that we might want to wait a little while before I moved back into our bedroom."

"Where are you going to sleep, Cassandra? We only have three bedrooms in this house and they're all taken."

Wringing her hands and looking everywhere but at JT, Cassandra said, "I thought I would sleep in the room with Lily for a little while."

JT sighed as he let go of Cassandra's hand and sat down. He looked at his wife as he said, "That's not going to work for me, Sanni."

There had been a time when Cassandra had asked JT not to refer to her as Sanni anymore. That nickname meant a lot to Cassandra. It made her feel special and like she really mattered to JT. When he had done all his dirt, she no longer felt special, but times were different now.

"I don't plan to sleep in Lily's room forever. I just want to make sure this is going to work between us," Cassandra reasoned.

JT shook his head as he stood up and walked toward Cassandra. He put her hand in his. "I want a real marriage, and that includes you sleeping in here with me."

"But... but what if something happens? What if we can't make a go of this?" Cassandra asked with fear in her eyes.

"I know I let you down before, Sanni, but I'm a different man now. I will never hurt you like I did before."

What had Cassandra said to her mother earlier? Something about forgiveness being a choice? Maybe trust was a choice also. Maybe she needed to throw caution to the wind and just lean in. She wanted to forget about the past and move forward with JT as if nothing had ever gone wrong in their relationship.

When she didn't answer, JT said, "Have a little faith, baby. We are going to make this work."

Mattie was screaming inside Cassandra's head, telling her to look before leaping. She tried to deny the voices in her head and go with the feeling in her heart. "Okay, JT," she said. "We will have a real marriage." Cassandra then closed her eyes and allowed herself to be swept into JT's arms. She loved this man and wanted to spend the rest of her life making love to him. Cassandra silently prayed, *please, God, if this is a dream, don't let me wake up.*

OTHER EBOOKS BY VANESSA MILLER

The Blessed and Highly Favored Series is available in ebook format only . . .

The Blessed One: (March 2011) Joel Morrison proved his love for God when he lost all of his children in the 1952 Kern County earthquake, but never lost faith in God. He weathered those hard times, and God blessed him with five more children. But now that his children are grown and living their own lives, Joel worries that the devourer has once again set his sights on the family that God has blessed.

For the most part, Joel's children are successful and rich, yet very unhappy. Joel realizes that giving his children more money will not make them happy, nor will it secure a place in heaven for them, when their hearts and souls are not fully committed to Christ. So, Joel Morrison decides to change his will in an attempt to teach his children a lesson in giving. He invites his children on a family vacation in the Bahamas to tell them about a change to his will that will affect them all. However, Joel's declaration is not the biggest surprise of their vacation.

Shockwaves are sent throughout the Morrison family, the likes of which they may never recover from.

The Wild One: (release date: June 2011) Dee Dee Morrison-Milner is a movie star and the wild child in the Morrison family; you name it and she's done it, with almost no regrets. However, when her younger sister, Elaine, asks her to adopt an African orphan child (Natua), Dee Dee agrees because Hollywood is full of actresses adopting underprivileged children—it may help boost her career. But when a psycho fixates on Dee Dee's maternal abilities, she finds herself running from a stalker.

Learn how an ensuing tragedy involving the orphaned child brings restoration not only to Dee Dee and Drake's marriage, but more importantly, to Dee Dee's relationship with the Lord.

The Preacher's Choice: (release date: August 2011) Isaiah Morrison is a man after God's heart. Even though his wife divorces him, Isaiah continues to preach and declare the goodness of the Lord. He is content to live alone for the rest of his life, never imagining that God has something else in mind for him.

The first day Ramona Verse walked into Christ Tabernacle, she fell in love with everything about the church, and especially the handsome self-assured man behind the pulpit. But would a man like Pastor Morrison ever consider a woman with a dark past like hers? Ramona and Pastor Morrison are brought together through his need for someone to head his charity foundation, but Isaiah will soon discover that he needs much more from the secretive Miss Verse than he ever thought possible.

The Politician's Wife: (release date: October 2011) Eric Morrison's wife, Linda's issues with alcohol escalate and she hits a teenage boy while driving drunk. Eric covers it up and a very contrite Linda is now ready to atone for her sins. She finds the strength to stop drinking and gives her life to Christ. Eric is thrilled when his wife stops drinking. However, when she tells him that God wants her to start a Christian organization that helps recovering alcoholics put their lives back on track, Eric rejects the idea, convinced that it will put his bid for governor at risk.

When a blackmailer threatens to expose his wife's drunk driving accident and a media hound critical of his brother Isaiah's stop sinning and come to Jesus preaching style further threatens his run for governor, Eric must decide whether he will stand up for the truth that his father taught him and that his brother now preaches or sell his soul for public office.

The Playboy Redemption*:* (release date: January 2012) After a very public argument over increased child support payments, the mother of Shawn Morrison's third child is found dead. Shawn is the primary suspect. Now in a fight for his life, Shawn turns back to Lilly, the mother of his two other children, who never even received an engagement ring, and the woman whose heart he broke by cheating on her numerous times. Lilly is now a born-again Christian. Will her forgiving heart and new attitude concerning morality finally help Shawn turn back to God in this, his darkest hour?

Love Isn't enough (Short Story) ebook

Sometimes love just isn't enough and Hannah Ellison is sick of pretending.

She promised to love, honor and cherish her husband, but Thomas kept secrets. And now as Hannah wades through all of Thomas's unpaid bills, baby mama drama and her inability to conceive... she must decide if love is enough to keep her at home when her heart and mind is in turmoil over something that only God can fix.

This short story is loosely based on the Old Testament story of Hannah's plea for a child of her own (1 Samuel 1:1-2:26).

A Mighty Love (Novella) ebook

Shay Lamont was sick and tired of dating men who didn't know the first thing about being faithful. She'd spent a lifetime chasing after losers, now she was determined to spend the rest of her life chasing after God.

Just as Shay sets her sights on God, Malcolm Harris sets his sights on her... and Malcolm is just as determined to get what he wants. If Shay can let her guard down and learn to trust again, she just may discover the mighty love God intended for her heart only.

Long Time Coming

For complete list Visit www.vanessamiller.com

Faithful Christian Deidre Clark-Morris is a professional career-minded woman with a loving husband and beautiful home, but no children. Kenisha Smalls has lived in poverty her entire life and has three children by three different men. After learning that Kenisha has inoperable cervical cancer, the relationship between these two women becomes a catalyst of hope, leading them both to a place of redemption and healing.

AUTHOR BIO: VANESSA MILLER

Vanessa Miller of Dayton, Ohio, is a best-selling author, playwright, and motivational speaker. Her stage productions include: **Get You Some Business, Don't Turn Your Back on God, and Can't You Hear Them Crying.**

Vanessa has been writing since she was a young child. When she wasn't writing poetry, short stories, stage plays and novels, reading consumed her free time. However, it wasn't until she committed her life to the Lord in 1994 that she realized all gifts and anointing come from God. She then set out to write redemption stories that glorify God.

To date, Vanessa has written four complete series and one single title mainstream book. Her readership steadily grows with each new release as she is a consummate promoter of her works. Vanessa believes that each of her books touch the heart and soul of readers across the country in a special way. It is, after all, her God-given destiny to write novels that bring deliverance to God's people. These books have received rave reviews, winning Best Christian Fiction Awards and topping numerous Bestsellers' lists.

Essence Bestsellers' List March 2008; May 2008 (Former Rain)

Essence Bestsellers' List September 2008 (Rain Storm)

Black Expressions Book Club Alternate Selection
2007, 2008, 2009 & 2010

#1 Ebook for fiction on Amazon.com November
2010 (Long Time Coming)

#1 on BCNN/BCBC Bestsellers' List November 2010
(Long Time Coming)

Vanessa is a dedicated Christian and devoted mother. She graduated from Capital University with a degree in Organizational Communication. In 2010, Vanessa was ordained by her church as a minister. Vanessa believes that God has called her to minister through her writings and help readers rediscover their place with the Lord.

Most of Vanessa's published novels depict characters that are lost and in need of redemption. The books have received countless favorable reviews.

". . . Heartwarming, drama-packed and tender in just the right places."   **—Romantic Times** Book Review.

"Recommended for readers of redemption stories."
                                        —Library Journal.

Made in the USA
Charleston, SC
12 November 2015